THE
MOTIVE

THE
MOTIVE

Harry Carmichael

E. P. DUTTON | NEW YORK

For Dr. Wilfred Pearce—*in appreciation*

Library of Congress Catalog Card Number: 77-71330
ISBN: 0-525-16030-2
10 9 8 7 6 5 4 3 2 1

And the sea gave up the dead which were in it.

Book of Revelation

CHAPTER I

THE TWO-MAN CREW of police patrol car alpha-delta on the
A35 said afterwards that Robert Heseltine's tan Mercedes
overtook them as they were approaching Dorchester. Both
policemen remembered that the driver was wearing a light
check cap, metal-rimmed sunglasses and a linen jacket.

'. . . *Real good-looking car. You could tell it was almost
brand-new. And it had a registration number that sticks in
your mind*: RQH 1. *An expensive job like that is nearly
always privately owned . . .*'

There was nothing in the driver's behaviour to arouse
adverse comment. As the patrol car continued towards Dorchester the Mercedes went on out of sight.

The time was then a few minutes past nine o'clock in
the evening – a warm, still evening after another day of
unbroken sunshine. Beyond the Dorset hills the sky was
still tinged with the last fading glow of amber and rose.

At nine-fifteen a petrol pump attendant saw the hand-
some Mercedes going past. It was heading in the direction
of Winterbourne Abbas. He noticed it particularly because
the car was travelling without lights ten minutes after
lighting-up time.

'. . . *I saw another vehicle flash its lights at him but he
paid no attention. He still had his sunglasses on and I remember thinking he'd forgot he was wearing them. Now I
know he had other things on his mind. Makes you wonder
if anyone in a state like that really knows what he's doing
. . .*'

The man in the check cap and linen jacket drove steadily
towards Winterbourne Abbas along the highway that had
once been a Roman road. Soon he came in sight of the
little town.

Several cars passed him. One sounded its horn repeatedly

before he realized he was driving without lights. That was just outside Winterbourne Abbas. He switched them on as he was rounding the last bend.

A cyclist riding to the Saxon Arms had reason to remember RQH 1. He told his friends in the taproom that he had nearly been knocked down by a big shiny car that went past so close anyone would have thought the driver had not seen him.

'. . . *Some of these fellows behave as if nobody had any right to be on the road. Forced me almost on to the pavement, he did. Lucky for me I managed to get out of his way or I wouldn't be here now . . .*'

Only one other person remembered seeing the tan Mercedes that night. But that was when it had nearly completed its journey.

Four miles beyond Winterbourne Abbas the A35 became a dual carriageway. After another mile the car swung on to a minor road and headed due south to Compton Eagle.

From that point the route twisted and turned and made several sharp bends before reaching Long Mallet. Not much further on the road became little more than an unmade track.

A woman taking her dog for a walk called it to heel and kept well into the hedge to let the Mercedes pass. In the light of the moon the car came close enough to give her a good look at the driver. When questioned later she was able to describe the incident in detail.

'. . . *He didn't seem to notice me. I'll swear he wouldn't have stopped even if he'd run me over. He was wearing a light-coloured jacket and a check cap with a peak shielding his eyes and he just sat there staring straight ahead with both hands on the wheel. Gave me a nasty feeling. It's a lonely spot at night and you get some queer thoughts. I could've imagined he was dead and the car was going on by itself . . . if you know what I mean . . .*'

She came out on to the narrow cart-track and stared

after him until the car reached another bend that twisted hard to the right. If he had looked in the mirror he would have seen her standing erect in the moonlight with the dog crouched at her feet.

To him the woman and her dog were of no importance. One thing filled his mind to the exclusion of all else. Soon he would reach the end of a nightmare journey. Soon it would be over.

Now he could see Little Mallet on his left – a handful of whitewashed cottages hardly worthy of being called a village. On the map in the glove compartment it was represented by five or six tiny black dots.

He saw lights twinkling in the distance as the car went rushing along the rutted track between tall dusty hedges. He knew that people might be asking themselves where he could be going when only the sea lay before him.

What people said or thought was immaterial. All that mattered was what had to be done.

The last mile ran straight except for one short zig-zag with the banks on either side creating a series of blind corners. Then the track ended at a T-junction.

To left and right wound a footpath which followed the line of a cliff twenty yards ahead. Coarse grass fringed the cliff top. Down below the waters of the English Channel ebbed and flowed in the light of the moon.

Far out to sea the navigation lamps of a small craft were like stars floating on the water. Closer inshore the moon laid a causeway of silver tapering into the distant reaches of the night.

At a walking pace he drove across the footpath and on to the grass. The car bumped and lurched over the uneven ground until it was barely a dozen feet from the edge.

There he stopped, switched off the lights and got out. As he walked step by step until he was poised on the brink he told himself no one would ever know his innermost thoughts, the struggle that had been warring within him for so long.

This was the moment of truth. He still had time to change his mind . . . but only a very little time.

Sixty feet below the place where he stood alone in the moonlight, the tide rose and fell restlessly, wave upon wave surging over a jumble of slimy rocks at the water's edge. That was the only sound he could hear in all the vast expanse of sea and earth and sky.

Still time to go back . . . Soon it would be too late. Yet he had no choice. Death was the only escape.

All along he had known that this time had to come. Now it was here.

No choice . . . no choice . . . The waves heaved over a rocky ledge, climbing high and then receding again and again, with a sound like the recurring echo of the words in his head. *No choice . . . no choice . . . no choice . . .*

Lynn would be upset. Even if her feelings were more of guilt than grief she was bound to be upset. It was only natural.

But no woman could go on grieving for the rest of her life. She was young and attractive. Some day she would remarry. Until she did she would have no financial worries. The insurance money alone would see to that.

Strange how he could think of her without any emotion. There had been a time . . . but that was long ago. Now she was merely a woman he had known far back in the past.

It would have helped him salvage a little self-respect if he could have felt she was being spared humiliation. But Lynn had no part in this shabby affair.

The truth had to be faced. He was not doing it to protect her. One thing and one thing only made it imperative. He could not allow himself to be degraded. Anything was better than being professionally ruined.

This was the only way to freedom. The sea would resolve all his problems. He had no need to be afraid.

People might say he was mad. Men who had reached his position never did a thing like this. They always found another way . . .

It made little difference what people said. No one would ever tell them why it had been necessary. Their opinion meant nothing to him or to anybody else.

Nothing mattered now. There was no road back.

A cloud moved slowly across the face of the moon and darkness spread all around him. He had an odd feeling that this moment would never come again. This was the sign he had been waiting for.

In the dark he had courage. In the dark he could at last yield to the inevitable.

He wondered hazily why he went on thinking when there was no longer any need to think. The time for asking questions was over. Yet he had to do what so many men had done when they were about to die. It seemed important to understand what had motivated them once they made their final decision.

Some men left a farewell note. They wanted the world to believe they were perfectly sane and knew exactly what they were doing. Perhaps a man was entitled to that last vanity : defying people to say the balance of his mind must have been disturbed.

But not in this case. The world could think what it liked about Robert Heseltine. It would make no difference . . .

Minutes later the moon came out from behind the drifting bank of cloud. Darkness fled across fields and hedges and narrow twisting roads.

In the silver moonlight there was nothing to be seen on the edge of the cliff except a neatly folded linen jacket on which rested a check cap. Further back stood an empty car, registration number RQH 1. The driver's door was wide open.

Among the rocks far below, the waves played with something limp and shapeless until the tide began to ebb. Then the sea carried its burden into hidden depths where the light of the moon could never reach.

CHAPTER II

ON SUNDAY MORNING, August 21, Quinn of the *Morning Post* got out of bed late. His head felt as though filled with cottonwool, his mouth tasted of stale beer and tobacco. He had only confused recollections of the previous evening that had stretched into the small hours.

As had happened so often he had met a man who knew a man who knew another man. In the event they had all gone to the home of somebody whose name Quinn was unable to remember.

Dimly he recalled that too many people had been crammed into too small a room full of noise and smoke and exuberant laughter. Judging by his symptoms the morning after he had drunk too much and smoked too many cigarettes. Above all, he had talked even more nonsense than usual.

. . . Given the slightest encouragement you think you're the world's greatest wit. They laughed at your jokes because they'd had a skinful. In their boozy state they'd laugh at a TV situation comedy. You'll never learn . . .

Now he had overslept and he would have to rush. In his haste he cut himself while shaving and got blood on the collar of his pyjama jacket while he searched irritably for a styptic pencil that had disappeared from the place where he always kept it.

Eventually he stuck a scrap of paper on the cut to stop it bleeding. As he combed his limp, flax-coloured hair he studied himself in the mirror with distaste.

. . . Pasty face, jaded eyes, features that look as if you're half frozen. You could play the part of Dracula when he's just been dug up after a hundred years entombed in the ice. Better not let Mrs Buchanan catch sight of you on your way out . . .

He dressed hurriedly, knotted his stringy tie wrong way round and wiped his shoes with some crumpled toilet-paper. Then he went out on to the landing and closed his bedroom door softly. Below in the kitchen he could hear his landlady's complaining voice.

'. . . If he thinks Ah'm gaun traipsing up there to gie him a call he's mistaken. Ah'm no' surprised he canna rise at a respectable time in the morning. Comes hame at a' oors. Whaur he gets tae Ah wudnae like tae guess. Wan o' these days he'll come tae a bad end, that's for sure . . .'

In his efforts to tread quietly he nearly fell down the stairs and he knew Mrs Buchanan must have heard the noise. He hoped she would be too busy preparing breakfast to leave what she was doing and he would get outside before she discovered he had gone.

Her usual lecture on the evils of his ways would keep. He knew it all by heart. Listening to her was no cure for a hangover. Shame that she meant well. The trouble was she could never understand that repetition defeated the moral of her sermon.

Women of her type so often made the same mistake. They wanted to change him solely for his own good. Maybe that was why he had never married. The thought of years of improvement stretching endlessly into the future was too much.

'. . . I don't think such a lot of me as I am but I wouldn't be able to live with the kind of remould I'd become by the time they'd finished with me. If she likes me enough to go to constant trouble on my behalf why doesn't she leave me alone? I am what I am – an ill-favoured thing but mine own, as Touchstone said . . .'

Mrs Buchanan was waiting for him in the lobby. With her hands folded over her massive stomach, she asked, 'Were ye thinking of gaun oot withoot yer breakfast, maybe?'

'I don't want anything to eat,' Quinn said. 'Thanks all the same but I'm not hungry.'

'Ye hae nae need tae thank me. Ah'll no' be caring if ye kill yersel'. When the likes of ye gae withoot there's a' the mair for the rest o' us. Ma only worry is we'll find ye deed wan o' these days.'

'That day is a long way off.'

'Is that a fact? By the looks o' ye I'd say ye were hauf deed a'ready. Hae ye taken a guid look at yersel' lately?'

Quinn said, 'Not five minutes ago. What d'you think put me off my breakfast?'

'It's nae laughing matter.' Behind the impatience in her voice she was unable to hide her motherly concern. 'Wi' a' yer drinking and the scandalous oors ye keep only the guid Lord kens how ye can dae yer work.'

'I'll have no work to do –' he opened the street door and grinned at her as he backed out – 'if I don't get on my way. See you when the coo caufs a cuddy . . . or words to that effect.'

'Ye talk real daft. Surely yer no' gaun oot afore ye've even had a cup o' tea?'

'I can get one at the office,' Quinn said. 'A hearty guid morning tae ye, Mistress B. As Rabbie Burns would say, Scots, wha hae wi' Wallace bled . . . and dinna get yer knickers in a twist . . .'

It was a warm bright morning with the promise of another hot day ahead. He thought it might be an idea to take a few days' leave while the good weather lasted. He had lost some of his zest for work in recent weeks and a break could be what he needed.

On the other hand, one pub was much the same as another. And that was where he would spend most of his time wherever he went. The only difference was that he would be among strangers.

. . . Pub friendship ends for the night when the landlord calls 'Time, gentlemen, please . . .' but it's comforting while you're inside the premises. Nice to have familiar faces

around you even if you wouldn't talk to them outside . . .

It seemed a long time since anything of real interest had occupied his attention. August usually had more than its share of dog days and this August was the worst he could remember. His Column on Crime was becoming more and more difficult to fill.

The glamour had gone out of criminal cases. People were surfeited with robberies, skinhead vandalism, youthful drug addiction, old women being assaulted and robbed of their handbags.

There was a sameness, almost a vulgarity, about the villainy he listened to in court. Even murder had lost its finesse. Now it was a matter of using a shotgun or bashing a security man over the head with a pick-shaft.

. . . No romance any more. A husband doesn't have to dispose of his wife by subtle means so he can be free to marry another woman. Divorce is now cheap, easy and relatively quick. Pretty soon it won't even be necessary. Marriage itself will be outmoded before long . . .

He told himself he was thinking sour thoughts because he had a sour liver. Some things changed but others were fundamental. It was too nice a day for cynicism. Aspirins and hot tea would restore his faith in humanity.

By the time his train reached Aldwych station he was in a better mood. Fleet Street always seemed different on a Sunday morning. The sky had more blue, the air less smell of diesel fumes. Maybe it was time he got some real fresh air and walked under a real blue sky. Maybe those few days in the country would be an idea.

When he arrived at the office he pushed thoughts of a holiday to the back of his mind. There would be time for that later. Not much fun going away on his own. Besides, his usual vacation was over-rated. Most times he needed a spell of convalescence when he returned . . .

It was earlier than he had expected. He took the lift to the canteen and had a mug of tea with a couple of slices of toast. After that he felt ready to face the new day. All he needed now was a cigarette before he began the day's work.

The man in Features studied him critically and said, 'You've been at the embalming fluid again by the look of you. If Mary Shelley were alive you could inspire her to write a sequel to Frankenstein.'

Quinn said, 'That's not the sort of greeting I expected from a colleague on such a nice day.'

'It was a nice day, it could still be a nice day. Only one thing spoils it. As the poet wrote: *Though every prospect pleases, and only Quinn is vile.*'

'Now you're being rude. Apart from the misquotation, he wasn't a poet, he was a parson who composed hymns – Bishop Reginald Heber. In their correct form those two lines are out of "From Greenland's Icy Mountains." Someone in your job should've known that.'

In a peevish voice, the man from Features asked, 'Have you quite finished?'

'Don't be ungrateful. I'm merely trying to improve your education. In return, you might lend me – '

'The answer's no. I don't smoke, I don't intend to smoke again and I haven't any cigarettes. Even if I had I wouldn't give you one. I know your idea of a loan. Besides, smoking's bad for you. You ought to get out of the habit.'

'This just isn't my day,' Quinn said. 'You're the second do-gooder who's given me a lecture. I've only to open my mouth – '

'Then try keeping it shut.'

With a wave of dismissal, the man from Features added, 'Same thing applies to the door behind you. Next time you pass this way, I'll be glad.'

'Is that your last word?'

'No, one more. Goodbye.'

'Lucky for you I have a forgiving nature,' Quinn said.

The noise in the reporters' room aggravated his lingering

headache. He ignored several facetious comments, scowled at somebody who asked him if he had got out of bed on the wrong side and told himself that too many people were too damn boisterous too early in the morning.

A dose of Aspirin was what he needed. He should have taken a couple before he left home or as soon as he arrived at the office. There was a bottle in his table drawer . . .

Like the styptic pencil, his Aspirins were not where they should have been. As he went on rummaging for them he remembered that he still had the scrap of paper sticking to the cut on his chin.

He moistened the paper until it came loose and then he peeled it off very carefully. In spite of his caution it bled a little. He held his handkerchief to it while he read the galley proof that had been propped behind the platen of his typewriter.

PUZZLE OF
MISSING LONDON
SURGEON

Dorset police began a search early today for Mr Robert Heseltine, consultant surgeon to the Brompton Clinic, London, following the discovery of his abandoned car on the cliffs south of Winterbourne Abbas. A linen jacket and a check cap were found nearby.

The car, a tan Mercedes, registration number RQH 1, was undamaged. There were no indications that Mr Heseltine might have been the victim of assault.

He was last seen shortly after nine-thirty Saturday night by a woman who lives in the village of Little Mallet which is only a short distance from the place where his car was found. She told the police he was alone.

A case containing various articles of clothing was on the rear seat of the car. A police spokesman said they had reason to believe that Mr Heseltine had arranged to spend the night at the home of a relative who lives in Dorchester.

Why he had driven to the spot where his car was found is not known. It is a sixty-feet drop to the sea below.

There was a scribbled note attached to the galley. Quinn scowled again as he unpinned it.

Local correspondent phoned this in while you were sleeping off last night's booze-up instead of earning your inflated salary. You might look into the affair – that is if it's not too much trouble.

Even if he had not recognized the handwriting he would have known who had written it. The news editor's brand of sarcasm was all too familiar.

On the surface he should hardly have been interested in what seemed a routine story. This fellow Heseltine was not the first man to drown himself because the pressure of living had become too great. His own particular reasons would become known in due course.

Quinn wondered why the local correspondent could not be trusted with the follow-up. There would only be the inquest. After that, both Robert Heseltine and the story would be officially dead.

Still . . . A professional man in Heseltine's position might provide a bit of human interest. Nothing else had come up of any use to Quinn's Column on Crime.

. . . Half a loaf in the hand is better than a rolling stone . . . as they say. Never can tell what you might dig up. Often the worst things are done by the best people . . .

He found his packet of Aspirins and chewed a couple of them while he did some more thinking. Then he went upstairs to the library.

'. . . Got any cuttings, Toby, on a bloke called Heseltine

— Robert Heseltine? He was an exalted member of the
medical profession until he parked his car near a cliff and
walked over the edge . . . or so it would appear.'

The librarian made a search in his files. When he came
back, he said, 'Nothing that I can find. Do you know anything about him?'

'Only that he was a surgeon who lived in, or near,
London. It's believed he drove to Dorchester for the purpose of visiting a relation but didn't. Instead, he turned off
somewhere and headed for the coast. There he took a high
dive off some cliffs into the English Channel.'

'Have they found him?'

'Not when our local man phoned in his story.'

Toby said, 'Chances are they never will.'

'You could be right. If so, the probate court will have to
presume his death.'

'That might be what he wants.' The librarian made big
eyes. 'Wouldn't be the first time a man made it look as if
he'd drowned himself when his real idea was to drop out of
the rat-race.'

'I envy your tortuous mind,' Quinn said. 'Got a large-
scale map of London to Cornwall?'

'For you – anything. What else would you like?'

'Last time a barmaid asked me that question I nearly got
my face slapped. I'll settle for your copy of the Medical
Directory . . .'

The route that Heseltine had probably taken was quite
straightforward. He would have gone from London via the
A316 to Staines, then used the A30 as far as Bagshot and
there joined the M3. At the end of the motorway the A30
led to Sutton Scotney . . . Stockbridge . . . Lopscombe
Corner and on to Salisbury where he would have followed
the A354 to Blandford, continuing south-west to Dorchester.

From that point to the spot where his abandoned car had
been found the most likely way was by Winterbourne
Abbas, then due south to Compton Eagle, west to Long

Mallet and south again to Little Mallet where he had been last seen.

Little Mallet to the cliffs overlooking the sea was only a short distance. Judging by the map, journey's end seemed nothing but a stretch of open country – more than two miles of high ground stopping abruptly above the waters of the English Channel.

If Robert Heseltine had not been familiar with the district he must have studied a map either before leaving London or some time in the course of his journey. That much was obvious. He could not have arrived at that particular place by chance.

A puzzling feature was why he had driven such a distance solely for the purpose of taking his own life. At a rough estimate, London to Little Mallet was a hundred and thirty to a hundred and forty miles. Even thirty miles of motorway would not reduce normal travelling time to much less than two and a half hours.

. . . And that doesn't include getting out of London proper. Fair amount of traffic on a Saturday evening around seven o'clock . . . if that's when he set off . . . if he drove straight from A to B without stopping . . .

Among other questions was whether Heseltine had been married and, if so, why his wife had not gone with him to visit the relative in Dorchester. That might explain a lot.

The biggest question of all was what had happened after he was seen by the woman who lived in Little Mallet. Perhaps the obvious answer was the wrong one.

His biographical details were not of much help. He had read medicine at Cambridge, gained his degree at the age of twenty-four and spent the next five years at a London teaching hospital where he became a registrar to a consultant surgeon.

From then on he had made rapid progress. Now he was Mr Robert Q. Heseltine, MSc, FRCS, with a string of honorary degrees after his name and a consultancy post at the Brompton Clinic.

. . . If he didn't walk off the top of that cliff. Otherwise he isn't anything. Shame to have such an illustrious career end in a verdict of Found Drowned . . . if he was drowned . . . and if he is found. At forty-seven he'd be in his prime. Might be a story here after all . . .

Quinn made a note of the route to Winterbourne Abbas and then went back to the reporters' room. After he had re-read the galley proof he rang the switchboard operator.

'. . . Any idea who our man in Dorchester might be?'

'Well, he might be Chou en Lai, General Amin or Sammy Davis Jnr. Personally speaking, I don't think he is but – '

'As a comic you have no future,' Quinn said. 'What's the fellow called?'

'Depends on which Dorchester. There's one in Canada, one in America and one in Dorset, England. If it's the town I think you mean . . . his name's Downey – Hugh Downey. He was on the phone earlier this morning. I put him through to Reporters'. The time he phoned is on record so, if you're interested, I can look it up for you.'

'I'm aflame with indifference,' Quinn said.

'Then I can't be of any further service?'

'Oh, but you can. I want to know his number. I also want you to get it for me. Understood?'

The operator said, 'You could at least say please . . .'

Downey was at home. He sounded young, keen and co-operative.

'. . . Just got back. Been out taking a look at the spot where they found the car.'

'Is it still there?'

'No. The police removed it by trailer. It's under cover now being checked for fingerprints and various other things.'

'Why?'

'According to them, merely routine.'

'Not because they know something they haven't disclosed yet?'

'I've no reason to think so. They provided me with all the details I used in my story. In a case like this they want as much publicity as they can get.'

Quinn said, 'I'd be surprised if they didn't. Do you know the name of the woman whom Heseltine passed near Little Mallet?'

'Yes. She's a Mrs Rose Lofthouse.'

'Have you spoken to her?'

'Didn't think I needed to. The police have told me what she says happened last night. Doesn't amount to very much, at that.'

'Let's hear it, anyway.'

'Well, she'd been taking her dog for a walk along the cliff path and was on her way back to the village when this big car came along – '

'From the direction of the village?'

'Nowhere else it could've come from. There's only one road passes Little Mallet to the cliffs – if you can call it a road. She says the driver behaved like a man who was either blind or drunk. If she hadn't grabbed her dog and got close into the hedge he'd have run over her.'

'Could she describe the car?'

'Not accurately. Doesn't know one model from another. But in general terms it answers the description of Heseltine's Mercedes.'

'How about colour?'

'Fawn or light brown or something of that kind. Tan isn't easy to distinguish by moonlight.'

'Don't suppose she got the car's registration number, either?'

'You're right . . . although I don't see why it matters. She says the driver was wearing a white or cream jacket and a check cap with a peak. From what she saw of him he looked like a zombie. Of course, I wouldn't have expected him to be grinning all over his face seeing he was on his way to jump into the sea.'

Downey paused. Then he asked, 'What's behind these

questions? Have you got some notion it wasn't the same
car?'

'No, merely fishing without bait and with a blunt hook.
You don't mind, do you?'

'Of course not, Mr Quinn. I'll be glad to tell you everything I know. Why don't you come down here and have a
look around for yourself?'

'If and when there's an inquest you can introduce me to
the local brew,' Quinn said. 'What are the possibilities of a
body being washed up in that part of the Channel?'

'Could take days or weeks. Maybe never. It was high tide
at nine-fifty last night. He might've been carried so far out
that the fishes will strip him to a skeleton and his bones
will lie on the bed of the English Channel for all time.'

'Charming thought. Now let's sing Yo-ho-ho, and a
bottle of rum.'

'It's true,' Downey said. 'There's no guarantee he'll ever
be seen again.'

'Is that just your opinion or do the police think so as
well?'

'In their experience it's not unlikely. Judging by previous
cases of drowning in that area anything might happen.
We'll just have to wait and see.'

Quinn said, 'Pleasant prospect for his wife. She never
knows which night somebody'll knock at her door and
say: Your husband's come home from the sea . . . tra-la-la.
Is there a Mrs Heseltine, by the way?'

'Yes. The police have been in touch with her.'

'What does she have to say about poor Robert's strange
behaviour?'

'Can't suggest any explanation. He was in a perfectly
normal state of mind when he left home to go to the Clinic.
Had to do a ward round and then he was going to lunch at
a local restaurant before setting off for Dorchester.'

'When was he supposed to be leaving town?'

'Some time during the afternoon. But he didn't manage
to get away. An emergency operation cropped up. Some

GP he knew had to have his appendix removed in a hurry and was scared of having anyone but Heseltine do the job.'

Once again Downey paused. He asked, 'Have you noticed how frightened so many doctors are at the thought of being cut open?'

'Maybe they know things they won't tell their patients,' Quinn said. 'However, I take it that Heseltine performed the operation.'

'Yes. He'd already told his aunt in Dorchester he'd be arriving in time for tea and he had to phone and explain he wouldn't get there until after nine o'clock. His wife says when he rang her he was a bit irritable over the upset to his arrangements . . . but consultants like to go along with the GP's wishes if they possibly can.'

'Because they know better than us peasants it's the GP who puts the jam on their bread and butter,' Quinn said.

'Perhaps so. Whatever the reason, Heseltine had lunch and went back to the Clinic. By that time his patient was ready to be taken down to theatre . . .'

With a hint of wry amusement in his voice, Downey added, 'You'll be glad to know the operation was successful.'

'I'm delighted. What time did Heseltine set off on his trip to the Dorset coast?'

'According to the theatre sister it would be close on seven o'clock. The police have spoken to her as well.'

'Which police are handling the case?'

'Dorchester. Detective-Superintendent Wainwright is in charge. He's quite a nice fellow.'

'For a copper,' Quinn said.

'No, I've always found him pleasant to deal with. Treat him right and you'll have few complaints.'

'I'll have none at all if he does the treating. Did this Mrs Lofthouse approach the police and tell them about the car that passed her on the road last night?'

'Yes. When she heard the news she thought they ought to know what she'd seen.'

'How did she get to hear so soon?'

'Milkman told her early this morning. He got it from the mother of a youth who'd been to some party or other in Lynchurch last night and he and a pal walked home to Little Mallet along the cliff top. They saw the car where there shouldn't have been any car and when they came across the jacket and the cap they got an idea something was wrong . . .'

'Then what?'

'Soon as they got to the village they phoned the police at Compton Eagle. The constable there went to take a look . . . and passed his impressions to CID at Dorchester. That's the lot.'

Quinn said, 'Not quite. Has anyone asked why Heseltine's wife didn't go with him if he was visiting his aunt?'

'It wasn't a social visit. Her local GP has been treating her for some sort of complaint and decided two or three days ago he'd like a word with her nephew. They arranged to have a consultation at Mrs Lloyd's home on Saturday afternoon.'

'Postponed until late evening.'

'Yes. He wasn't expected to arrive much before nine-thirty.'

'In the event he never arrived at all,' Quinn said.

'And not likely to, either. Drove straight through Dorchester, turned off to the coast and parked his car damn' near the top of the cliffs. After that he just disappeared. Peculiar, isn't it?'

'Intriguing,' Quinn said. 'If I may use what's known as a journalistic gallicism. Had he booked a room for the night at a Dorchester hotel?'

'No. The original intention was that he'd stay at his aunt's house.'

'What does she have to say?'

'Don't know . . . but I should imagine she's rather upset.'

'Have the police spoken with her doctor?'

'So I understand. It was he who told them about the

consultation and Heseltine's phone call to postpone the time of their meeting. Seems the GP waited at Mrs Lloyd's house until eleven o'clock before deciding to call it a day.'

Quinn said, 'You're a fount of information. Ring me later in the day if there are any developments . . .'

He sat drawing doodles on his scrap pad while he tried to think of some reason why a man in Robert Heseltine's position should want to drop out of existence and what motive he could have had for doing it in this manner. There were more discreet ways . . . if he had wanted to use discretion.

. . . *You'd think he deliberately set out to attract the maximum publicity. A medical man doesn't lack the means to commit suicide when he gets tired of life . . . or scared of living. He doesn't need to set a dramatic scene. All he has to do is go to bed, swallow a few sleeping pills and wash them down with a stiff Scotch. All very nice and quiet. No fuss, no bother. He just falls asleep and never wakes up again . . .*

If it were a case of suicide, Heseltine had chosen not only a strange place but also a strange time. After a busy professional day he had made a two-and-a-half-hour journey to a town where he had an appointment he had no intention of keeping.

The whole situation was illogical. Unless something had happened on the journey . . . unless the weight of a terrible problem had unbalanced his mind . . . unless a sudden fit of insanity . . .

One of the doodles became a primitive drawing of a car on a cliff top with the sea down below. A little matchstick man, arms and legs outstretched, was falling headlong towards the water.

For a long time Quinn sat looking at it, his thoughts chilled with the emotions of the man who had been about to die. Yet behind his thoughts he still wondered if this was what people were meant to believe. The setting was just too complete. He had read this kind of thing a hundred times.

A man went down to the water's edge, removed his outer clothing and walked into the sea until he was out of his depth. Then he emptied his lungs and let himself sink.

It could happen to any man. A high court judge had once taken his own life. The exalted as well as the lowly sometimes found the weight of the world too great.

But it would be rare with someone like Robert Q. Heseltine, MSc, FRCS. Married, successful, respected and prosperous . . . he was hardly the type.

One reason could make it feasible. If he had been told recently that he was suffering from an inoperable malignant disease, he might well have decided to avoid the terminal degradation that would serve no purpose other than to demonstrate his ability to withstand suffering.

Feasible . . . But someone must know if it were based on fact – someone probably at the Brompton Clinic. More than likely Heseltine had not told his wife. If he had received the report himself only that day . . . if . . . if . . .

A colleague would know. Heseltine could not have carried out his own investigation. But if his body were not found, the colleague was under no obligation to reveal that Heseltine had not long to live.

All of which assumed so much. Quinn told himself that, if the assumptions became facts, there would be nothing he could use in his Column on Crime. Nowadays few people looked on it as a crime to commit suicide. Maybe that might be worth writing as a special feature. It would certainly stimulate plenty of correspondence from readers.

He got rid of the piece of scrap paper, went upstairs again to the canteen and had another cup of strong tea. Then he decided to dump his problem on somebody else's lap.

CHAPTER III

THE NEWS EDITOR sucked the cap of a ballpen while he listened, his pale bulbous eyes without any expression. When he had heard it all, he asked, 'Well, what d'you want me to do? Write it for you?'

Quinn said, 'That'll be the day. You lack the necessary touch of genius. What I want is advice. Whenever I'm in doubt am I not supposed to consult the oracle?'

'This isn't an advice bureau. If you can't do the job you're paid to do why don't you resign?'

'It's not so much that I can't as whether I should . . . as the bishop said to the actress. The Heseltine affair doesn't seem proper material for my column.'

'Why not?'

'Because it hasn't any element of crime.'

'You're losing your touch,' the news editor said.

'How so?'

'For a man with your experience it should be obvious.'

'To a man of experience, nothing's obvious. Tell me why it looks that way to you.'

'All right. Robert Q. Heseltine, MSc, FRCS, couldn't have reached the heights of his profession if he'd suffered from lunar madness which eventually drove him to commit suicide that night because there was a full moon. So what else would make him do it?'

'You're supposed to be telling me,' Quinn said.

'By a process of elimination, I will. Here we have a professional man who's well-fixed, a pillar of the community, in good health and happily married . . . so far as we know. Does he sound the type of medical gent who'd drive close on a hundred and forty miles to jump into the sea with his clothes on?'

'Correction. He'd taken off his cap and his linen jacket.'

'A mere quibble. If he went to that place – all the way from home – for one specific purpose and – '

'He didn't make the journey just to drown himself. He was visiting his aunt's house to have a consultation with her GP.'

'But he didn't go there. Instead, he travelled miles beyond Dorchester without stopping. Why? What made him change his plans and do a crazy thing like that?'

'You're saying he must've blown a fuse,' Quinn said.

'Well, he wouldn't do it unless he had no way out. A man doesn't take his own life when he's sitting on top of the world.'

'Which could mean Heseltine liked being at the top but somebody wanted to bring him tumbling down.'

'I hadn't thought of it that way. Maybe the idea's worth kicking around.'

'What idea?'

'Let's start with blackmail.' The news editor looked pleased with himself. 'It's as good a place as any.'

Quinn said, 'Not to me, it isn't. First you'll have to suggest something he'd done that he wouldn't want people to know about.'

'With a man in the medical profession that could be any one of a dozen misdemeanours.'

'True enough. But if he did have a skeleton in the cupboard, how come it didn't start rattling until he was on his way to Dorchester? He doesn't seem to have been disturbed about anything when he left the Brompton Clinic as late as seven o'clock.'

'Appearances can be deceptive,' the news editor said. 'My opinion is that something happened at the Clinic yesterday – something that might've been simmering for a long time but suddenly boiled over. If I'm right you've got yourself a real juicy story.'

He sat up, tucked the end of his tie inside his trousers, and added, 'Now I'm not going to let you pick my brains any more. So buzz off. The audience is at an end.'

Quinn said, 'Just one thing more. You mentioned that I was losing my touch and it reminded me – '

The news editor pointed a long forefinger. He said, 'I haven't any. I've stopped smoking – thanks to you. On my salary I can't afford to buy cigarettes for both of us. Out!'

There was no phone call from Hugh Downey that day. His story that Quinn had read in galley proof went into next day's *Morning Post*.

On his way home Sunday night Quinn re-read the account twice. He thought about it over his evening meal, answered Mrs Buchanan's talk with monosyllables and went up to bed earlier than usual.

For an hour he lay awake thinking all round what he knew about a man called Robert Q. Heseltine. It was very little . . . apart from those biographical details in the medical directory. And they all referred to the past – the distant past. Much more important was what had happened to him during the previous twelve hours.

Breakfast to bedtime, Saturday, August 20 . . . crisis day in the life of a man who had everything to live for. Either he was dead or he had deliberately arranged to make people think he had jumped off the cliffs near Little Mallet.

If he were still alive, the question was why he should have wanted to fake his own death. Money could scarcely be the answer.

Yet it had to be one way or the other. And neither way made sense.

. . . *Even if He-Who-Must-Be-Obeyed is right and black-mail is behind it all, I don't see why he had to drive best part of a hundred and forty miles just to drown himself so that nobody would find out he'd been up to some mon-key business. In addition, a man with a load on his mind is bound to show it. But apparently theatre sister didn't notice anything strange in Heseltine's behaviour during the opera-tion or when he was setting off for Dorchester . . .*

Moments of illusion came between Quinn and his wandering thoughts. He roused himself with difficulty, made a mental note to call at the Brompton Clinic as soon as there was any news from Downey, and then surrendered his mind to sleep.

Time provided the answer to every problem. Tomorrow was far away . . . tomorrow, and tomorrow, and tomorrow . . .

Those lines by Macbeth: '. . . *And all our yesterdays have lighted fools the way to dusty death . . .*'

Someone else had once written about a watery grave. That fitted better. There was no dust below the cliff where Robert Heseltine had parked his car and then walked into oblivion.

As Quinn fell asleep he took with him the picture of a place he had never seen. Most details were hazy but one thing stood out sharp and clear. Like a sky-diver in a delayed parachute drop, the matchstick figure hung suspended above the sea.

He awoke before seven o'clock and was downstairs by seven-thirty. Mrs Buchanan had already laid out the breakfast table.

With her hands on her hips she looked at him. She asked, 'Hae ye fell oot o' bed? Whit brings ye doon afore they've aired the pavements?'

'Great minds don't need much sleep,' Quinn said. 'Napoleon, for instance – '

'Ah hae nae time for ony havering. Sit doon and haud yer wheesht. The day's gaun tae come when ye'll need that breath . . . tak it frae me.'

Over breakfast he glanced through his copy of the *Morning Post* again. When he got up from the table, Mrs Buchanan said, 'Ye've had mair tae eat the day than a' last week pit thegether. Hae Ah no' been telling ye it's gey bad gaun tae bed wi' a bellyfu' o' beer?'

Quinn said, 'Ye hae an' a'. Whit aye keeps me in a

swither is why ye dinna gie it up.'

As she raised a threatening fist, he added, 'Let's no' hae a rammy, Mistress B. Ah must awa' the noo, ye ken forbye, Ah must awa 'the noo. And when we meet again, ye ken, Ah'll no' be fou. Ah'll just hae had a drap or two.'

He went out hastily. On his way along the lobby he was singing to the tune of the 'Cock o' the North' : 'Aunty Mary had a canary up the leg of her drawers, Auntie Mary had a canary . . .'

At a quarter to nine there was no one else in the reporters' room. He spent five minutes on the other daily papers, read several accounts of what had happened at Little Mallet and learned nothing new. Their stories were materially the same.

He wondered if it would serve any purpose to have a chat with Detective-Superintendent Wainwright of the Dorchester CID. After some thought he decided against it. There would be plenty of time for that later. At this stage nothing had changed since the Mercedes was found abandoned.

Mrs Heseltine would probably refuse to talk to him. She was entitled to be distressed and in no mood to answer questions. His best prospect would be to ask somebody in Robert Heseltine's profession . . .

Dr Young had only just arrived at his surgery. He said, 'My waiting-room is filled with suffering humanity all of whom know I don't start healing and comforting the sick until nine o'clock. You'll have to take your turn and – '

'You won't get me in your waiting-room,' Quinn said. 'I'm in good health and I intend to stay that way.'

'Oh, so that's how we feel this fine summer's morning, is it? If you don't need my ministrations, just what do you want?'

'Information about a certain Robert Q. Heseltine with whom you may have had professional dealings.'

'Heseltine? You mean the consultant surgeon?'

'That's the man.'

'Why are you interested in him?'

'I'm interested in lots of people. I look upon all the world as my parish.'

'Don't quote John Wesley to me so early in the day. What is Heseltine supposed to have done?'

'Disappeared. And there's no supposed about it.'

'How disappeared?'

'Well, all the indications are that he jumped off a cliff in Dorset and drowned himself.'

'Jumped off a cliff . . . I don't believe it. Where did you get this cock-eyed story?'

Quinn said, 'Since I wasn't there I didn't see him do it but it's in several of today's papers. My job is to find out what reason he might've had for taking his own life.'

The phone was silent. Then Young asked, 'Why Dorset?'

'That would take too long to explain. In any case, the explanation isn't very satisfactory. It'll save time if we skip it. Tell me instead what you know about him.'

'Not all that much. I've sent a number of my patients to him and we've had the usual consultations. Likeable fellow and competent at his job. Always had a good reputation. Can't understand why he'd do a thing like that.'

'Neither can anyone else. What about his social life?'

'The kind you'd expect of a man in his position. Belongs to the right clubs and mixes with the right people. Kept busy most of the time and lived a pretty full life, I'd say.'

'Money?'

'If I were to guess his income I wouldn't imagine he could ever be short of cash. Between his private fees and his salary from the Ministry of Health he'd have fifteen thousand a year, at the very least.'

'Gamble at all?'

'That I wouldn't know . . . but I doubt it.'

'Any gossip about his home life?'

In a changed voice, Dr Young said, 'Now you're treading on dangerous ground.'

'How so?'

'The man in question isn't officially dead – merely disappeared. I've no wish to be sued for slander if he turns up again.'

'Does that mean you're aware of something that could give rise to gossip?'

'No, it doesn't. It just means I'm not prepared to discuss the man's private life . . . or any other man's private life, for that matter. Now you'll have to excuse me. I'm needed to preside over the daily charade.'

'Just another minute,' Quinn said. 'Did you ever meet Heseltine socially?'

'As it happens, I have done on a couple of occasions. He is, or was, a vice-president of the Metropolitan Medico-Legal Society of which I'm a member. We have guest speakers now and again and round off the evening with coffee and biscuits. Incidentally . . .'

'Well?'

'A pal of yours is also a member of the Society. You've written about him once or twice in your column and the last time we met I mentioned your name. According to him he's known you for years.'

'Who is this pal of mine?'

'A man called Piper – John Piper.'

'How does he come to be a member of this Society? He's neither a doctor nor a lawyer. He's an insurance assessor.'

'Oh, we have a sprinkling of outsiders. Helps to preserve our sanity. We only draw the line at newspapermen.'

Quinn said, 'I'll ignore that. Be useful if Piper and Heseltine mixed socially. I might learn something of Heseltine's domestic affairs.'

'Would your friend Piper confide in you?'

'I'd be surprised if he didn't. He knows I never betray a confidence.'

'Then I'll give you a tip that'll save your time and mine.'

'Such as what?'

'Ask him,' Dr Young said. 'If it does nothing else it'll get you off my phone . . .'

By nine-thirty the reporters' room was coming to life.
Quinn borrowed a cigarette, coughed over the first lungful
of smoke and sat wheezing until he recovered his breath
with difficulty.

Someone remarked that the blotched look on his face was
an improvement. '. . . Adds a touch of colour to these drab
surroundings. When you choke to death one of these days I
think we'll have you stuffed. Mounted on a plinth for all to
see, you'd serve as an Awful Warning on the evils of tobacco.'

Quinn said, 'Every time you open your mouth I'm convinced your parents never got married . . . and it shows.'

For the next half-hour he kept looking at the clock on
the wall. Hugh Downey would be phoning soon. There
were bound to be some developments. Even if police
inquiries had so far proved negative, that in itself would be
news . . . enough to keep the story alive.

It was now twenty-four hours since Downey had talked
to him. Something of interest must have happened in that
time. By now quite a lot would be known of Heseltine's
background. If he had reason to take his own life or to stage
this kind of disappearance, his reason could not remain
secret indefinitely.

At ten o'clock Quinn's phone rang. The operator said,
'Call for you . . .'

The line was noisy with interference. When it cleared,
Quinn recognized a familiar voice.

He said, 'You're the last person I expected to hear from.
How are you?'

'Oh, I'm fine. You keeping all right?'

'I've no cause to complain – although I frequently do.
It's the one liberty still retained by the peasants of England.'

'You never change,' Piper said.

'Ah, but all around me does. If Scott could see us now

he'd alter that bit in his "Lay of the Last Minstrel" : *This is my own, my native land.*'

'Why would he? This is still the best country to live in. However, what I really wanted to talk about – '

'You ask a question but you don't wait for the answer,' Quinn said. 'Nevertheless, I'll tell you. I think he'd re-write like this :

> *Breathes there the man, with soul so dead,*
> *Who never to himself hath said,*
> *This is my own, my native land.*
> *Now to himself he can but groan,*
> *'Tis native, yes, but not my own.*

Piper asked, 'Have you finished?'

'Well, yes. The muse has – '

There Quinn had another fit of coughing. It took some time before he got his breath back.

Then he said huskily, 'I was going to say the muse has deserted me but maybe I'm about o desert the muse. To what do I owe the honour of this phon call?'

'A story in today's *Morning Post* about   obert Heseltine, the surgeon. I thought you might be able to ll in some of the missing bits.'

'Wish I could. Unfortunately it's all there. Th only thing missing is Heseltine himself.'

'Do the police believe he committed suicide?'

'They've no reason to believe otherwise . . . although nobody can say for sure until his body's found.'

'They're convinced he's dead?'

'Frankly, I don't know. I haven't spoken to them personally. I got all my information from our local correspondent in Dorchester.'

'Does that mean you're handling the story?'

'At the moment you might say I have a watching brief,' Quinn said. 'Mind telling me what your interest is?'

'I've known the man for some years. He was once very

kind to me and I'd hate to think anything's happened to him.'

'Did you get to know him when you became a member of the Medico-Legal Society?'

'No, quite a while before then. It was he who nominated me for membership. Since Jane and I got married we've seen a lot of Mr and Mrs Heseltine.'

Quinn said, 'You're the very fellow who can help me. What sort of man is, or was, Heseltine? I don't imagine you've had any experience of him professionally.'

After a moment's hesitation, Piper said, 'In actual fact, it was in his professional capacity that we met. It's a long time ago now. Seems to belong to a different world. Strange how I seldom think about it . . .'

'What's strange?'

'How my memory of that night has faded until I almost feel as though it happened to somebody else. And I thought then I'd never get over it.'

Quinn was annoyed with himself for re-opening an old wound. He should have had enough sense to realize that Piper was talking about the loss of his first wife. When he remarried it was for him like being reborn. The ripples created by Heseltine's disappearance were already affecting the lives of others.

'You can't go on carrying a cross for the rest of your life,' Quinn said. 'I don't want to preach . . . but Ann does belong to a different world in a different time. My apologies for touching you on a sore spot.'

'No need to apologize.' Piper's voice changed. 'It doesn't hurt like it used to. The one thing I can't ever forget is that I was responsible for her death.'

'That's a load of rubbish. Your car skidded on an icy patch of road. However tragic the consequences it was just an accident.'

'Yes, but unfortunately I was driving the car. That's why I couldn't forgive myself.'

'Because you had a guilt-complex about the whole affair.

The law said you weren't to blame . . . nobody was to blame. But you insisted on wearing a hair shirt to atone for your imaginary sins.'

With an artificial cough, Quinn added, 'Here endeth the first lesson. Do you mind if I come back to this moment in time – to use a revolting phrase without which most trade union leaders would be speechless?'

Piper said, 'If you're talking about Heseltine there's not much I can tell you. He happened to be at the hospital that night and he did everything he could for Ann . . . although it was pretty hopeless from the start. Afterwards he took a look at me.'

'I didn't know you'd been injured as well,' Quinn said.

'Nothing serious. I had a fractured arm and one or two minor cuts and so on. Heseltine needn't have bothered with me but he could guess I was in a very low state and this was his way of showing sympathy.'

'Sounds like a nice fellow.'

'Oh yes. Always most considerate. I saw him several times in the next few weeks and we became friendly. Once or twice his wife invited me to dine with them and then he suggested that membership of the Medico-Legal Society might be good therapy. They had some interesting lectures that would help to get me out of myself.'

'And you remained friends,' Quinn said.

'Well, actually we saw even more of each other after I married Jane. I was able to return his hospitality . . .'

Piper hesitated and Quinn knew what he was thinking. The same unspoken barrier had stood between them for a long time.

. . . Both of us know what it's like to be the spare wheel on a bicycle. He ought to understand why I keep putting off those visits to his flat. It's all right for him to say Jane wonders when you're coming to see us. He knows as well as I do that two's company and three's an act of charity . . .

Then Piper went on '. . . Doesn't make sense to believe

he'd take his own life. What was he doing there in the first place?'

'He had no reason to be anywhere near the cliffs,' Quinn said. 'He was supposed to be visiting somebody in Dorchester.'

'Yes, I read that in the paper. Who was it?'

'An aunt whose doctor wanted Heseltine's opinion. What no one can understand is why he drove through the town without stopping.'

'How do they know he didn't stop?'

'Time factor. He left London around seven o'clock and a woman saw him between half past nine and a quarter to ten south of Little Mallet which isn't far from the place where his car was found. Judging by all the facts that have come to light he seems to have known where he was going . . .'

Piper listened without interruption. When he had heard the whole story he was silent for a while.

At last, he said, 'I can't make it out. No other news since you phoned your local man yesterday morning?'

'Not a word. In fact, when you rang me just now I thought it was a call from Downey.'

'Since he hasn't got in touch with you, seems obvious there's still no trace of Heseltine.'

'If he's in the sea he may never turn up,' Quinn said.

The phone went quiet again. Then Piper asked, 'What's your opinion? Do you think he has committed suicide?'

'Well, it looks that way. But before I'd bet good money I'd like to know something about his domestic life. Would you say he was happily married?'

'Without any question. I've known the Heseltines for a number of years and they've always seemed a very contented couple. Even if they'd had a row I can't imagine it would be so serious that he'd go and kill himself.'

'How about finance? Any trouble there?'

'I wouldn't give it a thought. In his position he'd have

no money problems.'

'If it wasn't money it must've been something equally compelling,' Quinn said. 'Do you think he's capable of staging a fake suicide because he wanted to disappear?'

'Nobody who's met him –' Piper sounded abrupt – 'would ever dream he could do a thing like that. There must be another explanation.'

'All right, suggest one.'

'That's what I'm trying to do. For his wife's sake I'd like to come up with some answer. I know the state of mind she must be in since yesterday morning.'

'Have you spoken to her yet?'

'No, I wanted to have a word with you first.'

'Well, now you know all I know . . . and it's not much. Why not see if Mrs Heseltine can be of help.'

'The police will already have questioned her.'

'But she might not tell them what she'd tell you. And maybe she could use your advice. What's wrong with going to see her?'

When he had thought it over, Piper said, 'If I do, I can't take you with me. You know that, I hope.'

'Sure. But you won't mind if I ask you what she has to say about hubby's strange behaviour?'

'It'll have to be in strict confidence.'

'Scout's honour. One thing you should bear in mind, of course.'

'What?'

'There are no secrets at an inquest,' Quinn said. 'Whatever made Heseltine do what he did it'll all come out in the wash.'

'If he's dead.'

'He'll have to do a lot of explaining if he isn't. Incidentally, would you say he's been a faithful husband?'

'That's not the sort of question I like to be asked. I've no reason to think that what's happened has anything to do with another woman.'

'It must have something to do with something,' Quinn said. 'Can you suggest a different reason?'

'I wish I could. One thing I'm sure of is that the answer won't be to Heseltine's discredit.'

'Your loyalty may be misplaced.'

'Not from my knowledge of the man. What do you propose to do at this stage?'

'First I'll ask Downey if there's anything new at his end. Then I think a visit to the Brompton Clinic is indicated.'

Piper asked, 'Do you know anyone there?'

'Not a soul. Do you?'

'Well, I've met one of Heseltine's colleagues. His name's Stone – Derek Stone. He's an ENT man. We were introduced at a Medico-Legal meeting.'

'All right if I mention your name?'

'If you think it'll do any good . . . which I doubt. Chances are he won't even remember me.'

'I'll take that chance,' Quinn said. 'Even if I get nowhere I have to try . . . as the bishop said to the actress. When do you think you'll be speaking to Mrs Heseltine?'

'Some time today . . . providing she agrees to see me.'

'Does that mean you've an idea she might not?'

'No, but she may be averse to having visitors of any kind.'

'Can't see why she'd want to sit alone at home worrying about her husband. You're the very person to give her some moral support.'

'If I had any to give,' Piper said.

'Play it by ear. A little soothing encouragement goes a long way. I'll ring you later in the day to see how you make out. If I learn anything at the Clinic we can swap notes. OK?'

'Yes, of course. But one thing puzzles me.'

'Lucky you. I've got a pocketful of puzzles.'

'This is about you, not Heseltine. Why are you devoting so much time and energy to an everyday affair?'

'What's everyday about this case?'

'Well, it'll probably turn out to be suicide.'

'You've changed your mind all of a sudden,' Quinn said.

'Not really. I've just come to the conclusion that nobody ever knows what's going on inside another man. Heseltine could've had all sorts of worries that I wouldn't be aware of.'

'Not all sorts. If a man otherwise sane finds himself driven to take his own life, I'd say we can narrow down the cause to one of two things – money or women.'

'Even supposing I accept that with reservations, it doesn't get us anywhere. Heseltine wasn't short of money and I doubt very much that he was involved with another woman.'

Quinn had a fleeting thought which left almost no impression. He said, 'You have a direct mind, my friend. In this case, just too direct.'

'I don't know what you mean.'

'You're not the only one. I've got an idea running around inside my head like a mouse and I can't catch it.'

'If you told me your idea I might be able to help,' Piper said.

'Too soon.' Quinn broke off to get rid of something in his throat.

Then he asked, 'Ever hear of a sixteenth-century dramatist by the name of Thomas Kyd?'

'No. And I don't see the relevance. Why you can't stick to the point – '

'Only thirty-six when he died, poor chap. Is believed to have written a pre-Shakespearean play about Hamlet. Bet you didn't know that.'

'My life isn't any richer because I know it now,' Piper said. 'What has Kyd to do with Heseltine's disappearance?'

'Nothing – personally. But one of his lines may be relevant: *For what's a play without a woman in it?* And I think there's a woman in this affair.'

'That's plain guesswork. What's happened to your old logical way of thinking?'

'The logical isn't always the obvious,' Quinn said. 'My guess is that this thing has a twisted sort of logic . . . like death itself. Bye-bye for now . . .'

CHAPTER IV

THERE WAS no call from Dorchester in the next half-hour. At a quarter to eleven Quinn decided he had waited long enough.

After some delay the switchboard told him Downey was out. '. . . He's expected back fairly soon. I've left word he's to ring you . . .'

Downey came through just before eleven o'clock. He said, 'No real developments. Fingerprint tests show that Heseltine was the last person to drive the car. All the usual things were in his overnight case and he'd also taken his medical bag. Pretty obvious what his intentions were when he set out.'

'But something made him change his mind,' Quinn said.

'Or he went out of his mind through overwork. Men in his profession are under constant strain. It's possible he just suddenly cracked up.'

'Is that what the police think?'

'Well, they haven't committed themselves one way or another . . . but the possibility has to be recognized. Not much good hunting a mare's nest when there's a simple answer to all your questions.'

'That makes two of you in one morning,' Quinn said.

'You don't agree?'

'Let's say I prefer to reserve judgment. I'll climb down off the fence when they find Heseltine's body.'

'Could be they never will.'

Quinn said, 'Never is a long time. Keep in touch. Wherever I am during the day, somebody here will know where you can get hold of me . . .'

An extensive car park with neat stretches of grass at either end fronted the main block of the Brompton Clinic.

Through a central archway Quinn could see modern additions to the original structure – single-story buildings linked to a glass and concrete block to form a new complex. Flower beds separated extra parking facilities marked out by white lines.

The inquiry office had a frosted-glass window and a bell-push : *Ring for Attention.* The window was open.

At a desk in the middle of the room a woman sat typing laboriously. She had short hair and a little crumpled face.

When Quinn tapped on the ledge of the window she looked up. She asked, 'Yes? Can I help you?'

Quinn said, 'I'd like to see Mr Derek Stone.'

'You want the Ear, Nose and Throat Department. If you follow this corridor until you come to – '

'I'm not a patient. This is a personal matter.'

'Is he expecting you?'

'Probably. I phoned his consulting rooms and his receptionist told me she'd do her best to speak to him before I got here.'

'M-m-m . . . I see.' The woman with the crumpled face retired within herself while she studied Quinn remotely.

Then she said, 'So far as I'm aware, Mr Stone is out. Would you care to have a word with his Registrar?'

'If he were on duty Saturday evening,' Quinn said.

Puzzled lines drew in the corners of her eyes. She said, 'I wouldn't know. In any case he won't be available until lunch-time. He's operating this morning. You'd do better to wait for Mr Stone.'

'Unless – ' Quinn could see no future in evasion – 'unless some other colleague of Mr Robert Heseltine is around.'

That puzzled her even more. She asked, 'Who is it you really want?'

'I was told to have a chat with Mr Stone, the ENT man,' Quinn said. 'But anybody who knows Mr Heseltine will do.'

'Lots of people know Mr Heseltine. What's this all about?'

If she had known she would not have asked. Quinn said, 'He's had an accident. It's important that I speak to one of his colleagues at the Clinic.'

Her eyes pretended to understand. She said, 'Dr Blake is somewhere in the hospital and so is Dr Egan. Would you like me to find out which one's available?'

'I'd be most grateful,' Quinn said.

She used the phone on her desk. He leaned against the window ledge and waited while she talked in a quiet voice to somebody called Alan.

'. . . Either of them will do. If Dr Blake's taking an outside call, see if you can get Dr Egan.'

With her hand over the mouthpiece she looked up at Quinn and asked, 'May I have your name?'

He said, 'Quinn – with a double N. You can mention that it was a friend of Mr Heseltine who advised me to come here.'

'Very well.'

Her eyes shifted from Quinn's face to the typewriter. As she sat listening, her mouth drawn in, he got the impression she disapproved of him.

A minute passed. He began to feel that this would be a wasted errand. These people never discussed their associates with an outsider. They were all members of a closed shop. If they knew who he was he would get the standard reaction – no comment.

. . . Funny that this woman hasn't heard about Heseltine. I'd have thought the news would've got around by now. Evidently hasn't reached her yet. Looks a bit like a Pekinese . . . not that you've any room to criticize somebody else's appearance . . .

Through his thoughts he heard her talking into the phone again. She said, 'Dr Egan? This is Inquiries. There's a Mr Quinn here who'd like a word with you about Mr Heseltine . . . yes, Q-U-I-N-N. Says he's been sent by a friend of Mr Heseltine . . . appears he's had an accident . . . yes . . . yes . . . oh, I see.'

She flicked a glance at Quinn. She asked, 'Will you speak to him, Dr Egan, or shall I tell him to wait until Mr Stone arrives?'

Once again she listened. Then she said, 'It was Mr Stone he wanted first of all but . . . yes, of course. Hold the line a moment, please.'

Quinn sensed a change in her attitude as she lowered the phone. She said, 'Dr Egan wishes to know who sent you and why he didn't come himself.'

'There's a simple answer to that,' Quinn said. 'He couldn't. He's calling on Mrs Heseltine this morning.'

'And his name?'

'Piper – John Piper. He's been a friend of Mr Heseltine for a long time and he's also pretty well known to Mr Stone.'

'I see.' She repeated the information into the phone as though she had little faith in it.

When she hung up, she said, 'Dr Egan will see you. He's in the Radio-Therapy Department. Follow this corridor as far as you can go and turn left. When you come to a sign that says Wards 12 and 13 there's a staircase to your right. It'll take you down to the basement where you'll see another sign . . .'

Quinn got lost twice in the busy corridors. Eventually he asked a passing nurse who took him part of the way and made sure he understood the rest of her directions.

Radio-Therapy occupied most of a long passage with pieces of wheeled equipment parked outside doors on either side. On one door there was a notice giving instructions in case of fire and warning of the hazards of radiation. Other doors were wired to devices that Quinn had never seen before.

A white-coated technician told him Dr Egan was in a waiting-room just round the corner. '. . . He asked me to look out for you. The card on the door says New Patients.'

'Glad you mentioned it,' Quinn said. 'I'd never have guessed that N-e-w P-a-t-i-e-n-t-s spells waiting-room. We live and learn . . .'

It was the first door on his left. He knocked once and walked in.

There were rows of chairs along two facing sides of the room and a low table in the centre littered with magazines and coloured supplements. Windows opposite the door let in the bright August sunshine.

Under one of the windows stood a man of more than average height with auburn hair and a smooth fresh complexion. He looked to be in his middle thirties – well-groomed, quietly dressed and with the air of the successful professional man.

In a voice that matched his appearance, he said, 'Mr Quinn? I'm Dr Egan. Please sit down and tell me what this is all about.'

Quinn said, 'If you don't mind, I prefer to stand.'

'As you wish.'

With a slight change of tone, he added, 'Since you want to talk about Mr Heseltine, I presume you know what's happened.'

'Only as much as you know,' Quinn said. 'Piper and I had a discussion earlier this morning and we thought it might be a good idea to see if the staff here could offer any explanation.'

Egan asked, 'Why? Isn't this affair best handled by the police?'

'No one's interfering with police inquiries,' Quinn said. 'From what I know of them they're only too glad to have any help they can get. Apart from which, Piper and Heseltine have been close friends for a long time.'

'So I believe. I've met John Piper at several Medico-Legal meetings. If I remember correctly, it was Heseltine who introduced us.'

In the same easy manner, Egan went on, 'I don't know you, Mr Quinn, but I have a feeling I ought to.'

It was the forerunner of a question that had to come once the preliminaries were out of the way. Quinn said,

'It's probably the name that's familiar.'

'Why? Have you been a patient of mine?'

'No, nothing like that. But if, like all the best people, you read the *Morning Post*, you'll have seen my Column on Crime.'

A different look came into Dr Egan's smooth face. He said, 'I'm surprised at John Piper thinking I'd talk to a newspaper reporter about this unfortunate business.'

'Don't blame Piper. He never mentioned you. It was Mr Stone's name he gave me.'

'Same thing. The situation's bad enough without inviting unwanted publicity.'

'You don't need to invite it,' Quinn said. 'And nothing you do can avoid it. What's more, I didn't create the situation . . . so it's unfair to treat me as if I were the villain of the piece.'

Dr Egan glanced down at his hands. When he looked up again, he said, 'I've no wish to be unfair. But let's be blunt, Mr Quinn. Your only interest is in getting a story for your paper. My concern is for Robert Heseltine. He's a friend as well as a colleague.'

'What I write will be the truth as far as it's known,' Quinn said. 'And the truth can't hurt your friend. You'll serve his interests best by preventing speculation.'

'That's a matter of opinion. All my experience teaches me that the least said the soonest mended.'

'Not always. If Heseltine's dead there's nothing to mend.'

'If?' A sombre look clouded Egan's face. 'Have you any reason to doubt it?'

'No. Frankly, I haven't. But, until his body's washed up, the possibility does exist.'

'A very faint possibility. Everything points – '

Dr Egan left the next word unformed. As he came away from the window he slapped his pockets as though to give his hands something to do.

Then he said gruffly, 'I'd rather not talk any more about it. The whole thing's very distressing. That's why I wish

Piper hadn't told you to come here.'

Quinn said, 'He didn't tell me. It was my idea. He only suggested that, if I were going to ask questions at the Clinic, I could mention his name when I spoke to Mr Stone.'

'Well, now you know my views on the matter, perhaps you'll go away.'

'I don't know your views – only your attitude. And it's different from Piper's.'

Egan frowned. He asked, 'How?'

'Because Piper rang me to find out what I knew. He's as concerned as you are but he's willing to talk about it.'

'What's there to talk about?'

'The motive behind Heseltine's actions on Saturday evening,' Quinn said.

'How do we know he had any motive?'

'That's as good as saying he must've been out of his mind.'

'No one –' Egan shook his head – 'no one can say that. I wouldn't even like to guess what happened.'

'Could he suddenly have gone crazy?'

'It would've had to be very sudden,' Egan said flatly. 'I still don't feel like discussing it with a stranger but, if you enjoy Piper's confidence, I suppose you can be trusted.'

Quinn said, 'We've known each other a long time and I haven't let him down yet. Anything that's confidential I keep to myself. And you needn't be afraid I'll quote you.'

'I'm not worried about that. I don't know anything worth quoting. All I can tell you is that Heseltine seemed perfectly all right Saturday afternoon.'

'When did you last see him?'

'Some time before six o'clock. I'd been here during the morning and I came back about five to take a look at a couple of patients who are under observation. Heseltine and I bumped into each other outside Number 3 operating theatre.'

'What did you talk about?'

'Nothing very much. I asked him what he was doing at

that hour and he told me he'd been taking out some GP's appendix. Sounded rather irritable.'

'Because he'd had to perform the operation?'

'Well, yes. It had upset his arrangements. He'd promised to be in Dorchester at half past five and now he wouldn't be there until late evening.'

'Apart from being irritable at the delay was there anything unusual in his manner?'

Dr Egan played with his hands while he thought. His eyes were blank and far away.

At last, he said, 'Perhaps I'm allowing subsequent events to exaggerate the impression I really got but when I look back . . .' He hesitated while he tried to find the right words.

Quinn asked, 'What impression did you get?'

It took Egan another few moments to frame his reply. Then he said, 'I didn't give it much thought at the time but I have a distinct feeling that Heseltine was worried.'

'About being delayed?'

'No . . . something else.'

'Any idea what it could've been?'

'Not a clue. And I might well be wrong.'

'Don't bet on it,' Quinn said. 'This sounds like the first real indication of Heseltine's state of mind before he set out to keep his appointment in Dorchester.'

Fretful lines marred the smooth skin around Egan's mouth. He said, 'I wouldn't be so sure. Being worried is one thing. But I can't see him deliberately taking his own life because he had some kind of problem. Heseltine's never been the depressive type.'

'Maybe. But people have been known to crack under pressure.'

'Only certain people. And nearly always there are warning signs. I've known Heseltine for years. Apart from our professional relationship we've met socially on many occasions . . . and I've never seen anything to make me suspect he was a man who could commit suicide.'

'Suppose – ' Quinn knew he had to put this very carefully – 'suppose Heseltine had only just learned he had something seriously wrong with him?'

With a changed look, Egan asked, 'You mean some organic disease?'

'Yes, the sort of thing that could be inoperable. It would depress even a man who wasn't the depressive type . . . wouldn't it? Certainly explain why he looked worried. Think the idea's worth pursuing?'

Dr Egan lost his air of indecision. He said, 'Not for a moment! You needn't give it a second thought. I'd have known if there'd been any investigation. He'd have asked me to arrange for X-rays and so on.'

'No possibility that he might not have wanted you to know?'

'None whatsoever. Not the slightest possibility. And, before you suggest it, he wasn't the sort of man to persuade himself he had some imaginary ailment.'

Quinn said, 'You know best. I'm not going to butt my head against a brick wall. So let's try another tack. Has there been any trouble here at the Clinic?'

With a shrug, Egan said, 'You can forget that, too. Heseltine's one of our most respected consultants. The staff, the Administration, the Regional Hospital Board – everybody has always had the highest regard for him.'

'No inquiries pending? No one questioning his competence as a surgeon?'

'If you mean was he worried because something had gone wrong during an operation, the answer's no. Anybody can make a mistake . . . accidents happen . . . but he's never blotted his copybook.'

Everything he was told only made Quinn all the more convinced that the reason for what had happened lay outside the Brompton Clinic. There had to be a reason. Heseltine's actions must have been inspired by some motive. Egan knew him well . . . and Egan could only say that

Robert Heseltine had seemed to be worried but not to any great extent.

One question chased another in Quinn's mind – questions that got lost in a no-man's-land of conjecture. Even conjecture got nowhere. What had taken place on the cliffs south of Little Mallet was itself in doubt.

Something had happened. Nobody knew what or why. The one established fact was that Heseltine had disappeared.

If there was a logical explanation, Quinn knew he would have to seek elsewhere. Nobody could have been more helpful than Egan but his information was almost entirely negative. The one positive thing was that he honestly believed Heseltine had not committed suicide.

... Perhaps he's mistaken. Perhaps he underestimates the effect of Heseltine's worry. But I know when a man's telling the truth and he's given me straight answers to straight questions. Egan can't think of any reason why Robert Heseltine should take his own life ...

Someone must hold the key to the riddle of what had happened between seven o'clock and nine-thirty on Saturday evening. How to find that someone was the problem.

Quinn asked, 'Did you tell the police that Heseltine had seemed worried when you met him outside the operating theatre?'

After a quick glance at his watch, Egan said, 'No. They never interviewed me ... and I had nothing tangible to justify approaching them. In fact, they'd been and gone before I learned they'd visited the Clinic.'

'You'll probably get another visit from them.'

'If we do, it won't achieve very much. You're no wiser now than you were when you came in here.'

'That's what I was just thinking. My job isn't going to be an easy one.'

'No job is easy. In this case you may finish up with little to show for your labours.'

'Won't be the first time,' Quinn said.

'Suppose not.' Egan looked at his watch again. 'Anything else I can tell you?'

'Doubt it. You wouldn't know, would you, if Heseltine was actually seen leaving the Clinic on Saturday?'

'As it happens, I do. When I read the story in my morning paper it was the first thing I asked soon as I got here.'

'And?'

'One of Mr Stone's team saw Heseltine getting into his car.'

'Alone?'

'Yes. There was no one with him when he drove out of the hospital grounds.'

'What time would that be?'

'Between twenty to and a quarter to seven.'

'Is he quite sure of that?'

'It's a she . . . Didn't seem in any doubt.' Dr Egan looked puzzled. 'Why?'

'Well, I got the impression from our man in Dorchester that theatre sister told the police it had been about seven o'clock.'

'Wasn't that a roundabout way of getting your information?'

'Maybe. The question is which of them is right.'

Dr Egan put both hands in his pockets, strolled to the window and stared out at the sunlit sky. His profile was thoughtful.

Eventually, he turned and asked, 'What makes you think it's important?'

'The time factor,' Quinn said. 'According to a witness near Little Mallet, Heseltine arrived there at roughly a quarter to ten. If he left the Clinic at a quarter to seven that would give him fully three hours for the journey.'

'And you consider it's too long?'

'Not necessarily. But, assuming traffic wasn't heavy, three hours would allow a small margin.'

'For what?'

'A break of perhaps ten or fifteen minutes between London and Dorchester,' Quinn said.

'M-m-m . . . I see what you're driving at.' Egan jingled the loose change in his pocket. It gave him time to think.

Then he said, 'Even if Heseltine did stop somewhere it might only have been to go to the toilet or have a cup of tea or – '

'Or make a phone call,' Quinn said.

Dr Egan looked even more thoughtful. It was easy to see that the idea had never entered his head.

He asked, 'Are you saying that Heseltine might've got a piece of disturbing news on the phone?'

'It's as good a guess as any.'

'Something so bad that it drove him to take his own life?'

Quinn said, 'Whether you relish the thought or not, it seems the only possibility. He could've been faced with a nasty alternative and he chose what he considered was the lesser of two evils.'

'I don't relish any part of this affair,' Egan said. 'But my regard for Robert Heseltine doesn't enter into it. The facts are all that count. And we've no facts to work on . . . or very few.'

'Granted. But if he hasn't committed suicide, where is he? What's happened to him? Why should a man who's sound in mind and body do what he did on Saturday night?'

'I – ' Dr Egan shrugged, his smooth face doubtful and worried – 'I don't know. Nothing makes sense. And I'm afraid I can't spend any more time talking about it. I've upset my schedule of appointments already . . . so you'll have to excuse me.'

'Of course,' Quinn said. 'Thank you for treating me so nicely. In the circumstances you were entitled to send me off with a flea in my ear.'

'Not at all. If there's any way I can help, don't hesitate to get in touch.'

As an afterthought, Egan asked, 'Would you like me to

find out if Mr Stone has arrived back?'

'I'd appreciate it if you would.'

'No trouble. There's a phone next door. Won't keep you long.'

With a quick nod he went out. Quinn passed the time sorting into some kind of order all the bits and pieces of information he had accumulated.

The evidence so far was that Heseltine had been alone at the beginning and the end of his journey. Something was also known of his state of mind before he left the hospital. Added to that was the possibility that he might have stopped on the way.

If he had . . . From that point Quinn wandered in the realms of theory with no facts to guide him. Perhaps Heseltine had made a phone call . . . perhaps he had met someone . . . perhaps the meeting had been pre-arranged . . . perhaps what they discussed had driven Heseltine to take his own life. Perhaps . . . perhaps . . .

In the events of Saturday evening lay the climax of a story that must have begun long ago. If Heseltine were dead, he had died because his life was forfeit – the price of what he had done or what had been done to him.

Theory drifted into fantasy. With an effort Quinn shook off the bizarre notions that crowded in on him. In all probability the answer could well be suicide for some reason that might never be uncovered. Chances were he was allowing his imagination to run wild . . .

Then Egan returned. He said, 'Sorry . . . you're out of luck. I did my best but Mr Stone says he never talks to reporters. Wasn't interested when I explained who you were.'

With a fleeting smile, Egan added, 'Told me he'd never heard of you.'

'Such is fame,' Quinn said. 'Deals quite a blow to my sinful vanity . . . if I had any. However, thanks all the same. It was good of you to try.'

'No, not at all. Doubt if you'd have learned anything

useful from him. He hasn't spoken to Heseltine since the middle of last week.'

'In that case I'll leave your Mr Stone to Piper.'

'That's probably best. Don't think it'll serve any purpose either way.'

A morbid look darkened Egan's face again as he went on, 'It's a bad business all round. I can imagine what this is doing to Heseltine's wife.'

Quinn said, 'Can't be pleasant for a woman not to know whether her husband's alive or dead. Wonder if she had any idea he might do something like this one day . . .'

CHAPTER V

IT TOOK Piper until nearly lunch-time to deal with his correspondence and make several phone calls. Monday was always a busy morning.

When he had finished dictating the last of his insurance reports, he sat for a while thinking of Lynn Heseltine and what he would say to her. They were on friendly terms but that did not entitle him to probe into her private life. At a time like this she might well prefer to be left alone . . . yet there could be no harm in a tactful inquiry by someone she knew and liked.

She answered the phone almost at once as though she had been expecting the call. Her voice was unsteady and he could guess what she was afraid she might hear.

He said, 'Hope I'm not disturbing you.'

'No . . . not at all. I just get scared any time the phone rings.'

'Of course. I can understand how you feel. Wish there was something I could do.'

'What can anyone do?' She sounded close to tears.

'There must be an explanation,' Piper said.

'If there is, I can't think of one. Robert was perfectly all right when he left home on Saturday morning.'

'So I understand. Something must've happened on his way to Dorchester. Would you mind if I tried to find out what it could've been?'

She hesitated for a moment. In an uncertain voice, she said, 'The police have assured me they're doing everything they can. I don't want you to waste your time . . . although I appreciate the offer. To be honest, I can't see how you can help.'

'I'd like to try, all the same. I've never forgotten that Robert was a good friend to me at a time when life was rather grim. Do you mind if I come out to Canon's Park and have a chat with you?'

Without any real enthusiasm, Lynn Heseltine said, 'You know you're always welcome. When can I expect you?'

'Soon after lunch. Is that all right?'

'Yes, of course.'

In the same downcast tone, she added, 'I'll be here whenever you come. I daren't go out. Someone may phone with news of – of Robert. I don't know what to do . . . I just don't know what to do . . .'

Piper could hear her crying as she hung up. The misery in her voice haunted him as he locked up the office and went downstairs.

Number 19 Martendale Crescent was a detached house situated at the arc of a horse-shoe of imposing residences. Trees in full leaf lined the pavements and the gardens were bright with summer flowers.

He parked five or six yards short of the double gates. As he walked up the drive he had not yet decided on the line his questions should take. Mrs Heseltine would only let him go so far. But the answer to her husband's disappearance might well depend on the depth of their relationship.

The house was very quiet. When Piper touched the bell-push he heard the two-tone chime echoing into the distance for what seemed a long time.

Then footsteps came near. He took off his hat and waited. At the back of his mind he remembered the last time he and Jane had visited this house and how different the circumstances had been.

Nice couple, the Heseltines. Always friendly and hospitable. Always made visitors feel at home. There had been many pleasant evenings in this luxurious home.

Now it had the air of a place empty and abandoned – a place which would never come alive again. Over it hung an atmosphere of grief as though Lynn Heseltine already knew that Robert was dead.

In spite of the warm sunshine slanting into the porch, Piper felt an inner chill. Perhaps she knew because she had reason to know. Perhaps the news of Robert's disappearance had come as no surprise . . .

The door opened. Lynn said, 'Hello. I'm glad to see you . . . I really am.'

She was slim, dark and elegant with sleek black hair like polished jet. Her lovely face was very pale. Piper saw in her eyes the weariness that must have grown more and more oppressive as the hours went by while she waited for the news she feared.

He wondered how he could have suspected that she had no need to be told. The look in her eyes could hardly be assumed. She was a woman who had lost hope. All she had left was a dread anticipation.

As she moved aside to let him come past, he felt a great sympathy for her. She had aged since they had last met. Then she had been an attractive, vivacious woman on the right side of thirty. Now she looked crushed with the weight of years.

Piper found himself thinking of the difference in age between Lynn and her husband. Robert was close on fifty.

. . . *Looks a lot less but he must be about twenty years older than she is. Not that the disparity in age ever seems to have harmed their marriage. A well-adjusted couple . . . if one can judge by appearances. Haven't seen them for several months but I can't imagine any change in their relationship that could explain what has happened . . .*

Mrs Heseltine led him into a small comfortably-furnished room looking out on to the garden at the rear of the house. It was enclosed by tall privet hedges high enough to ensure privacy. Around a trim lawn there were beds of standard roses in full bloom.

She invited him to sit down. '. . . Put your hat on one of the chairs and . . .' It seemed too much trouble to phrase the rest of the thought.

He watched her move here and there, her hands unable

to remain still, her eyes almost fearful. At the back of his
mind he wondered why she should be afraid of him.

After a long silence, she asked, 'What do you want to
talk about?'

Piper said, 'Anything you can tell me that you may not
have told the police.'

'Why – ' she imprisoned one hand in the other to restrain
its restlessness – 'why should you think I kept anything from
them?'

'That wasn't what I meant. Your answers to official questions aren't the same as talking confidentially to a friend.'

When she just stared through and beyond him, he added,
'At least, I hope you look on me as a friend.'

She roused herself from her apathy. She said, 'Of course
I do. I know I'm not behaving very well . . . and you'll
have to forgive me. I hardly slept at all last night although
I took something to make me sleep. Now my head feels as if
it's stuffed with cottonwool.'

'There's nothing to forgive,' Piper said. 'I'm here to be of
help. Use me in any way that'll take some of the load off you.

'Tell me how.' Her eyes were dry but there were tears
in her voice. 'Just tell me how. You can't bring Robert
back . . . and I know I'll never see him again.'

'You can't know that. It's too soon to assume the worst.'

'What else can I assume?'

'That depends on something I'm obliged to ask you.
There's no sense in being other than frank. Do you think
Robert has committed suicide?'

A fleeting look came and went in her eyes – a look that
drove out the fear which had never been far away. In a
small voice, she said, 'I – I don't know. I just can't believe
he'd do a thing like that.'

'Neither can I. But is it possible?'

She took a long time to answer. Piper could see the
struggle that went on before she made her decision.

Then she said, 'I wouldn't admit it to anyone else – and
the idea is still absurd – but it is possible.'

When he remained silent, she added, 'You won't repeat that, will you? I could be so wrong. And it would be unfair to Robert if people thought . . .'

Piper said, 'You haven't told me anything worth repeating. Besides, I have no obligation to tell the police what you say to me. Now, why should you think he might have taken his own life?'

Lynn Heseltine clasped and unclasped her hands while she stared into the distance. At last, she said, 'Because he's been under a lot of strain lately. In my opinion he was doing too much. I wanted him to take a holiday but he kept putting it off.'

She was evading the truth, in degree if not in substance. That was one thing Piper knew beyond any doubt. But to tell her she was lying would get him nowhere.

So he said, 'There's more to it than that, isn't there?'

'No – not really. A man doing his type of work –'

'Doesn't go and drown himself because he's been performing too many operations,' Piper said. 'You're his wife and you know him better than anybody else . . . that's only natural. But I've known him for a long time now and my opinion is that it would take more than overwork to make him commit suicide.'

She shook her head in protest. She said, 'It's months since you last saw him. He's not . . . well, he's not been himself recently.'

'In what way has he been different?'

'It's hard to describe. He's seemed . . . well, kind of withdrawn.'

'Have you asked him if he was worried about something?'

'I –' she avoided Piper's eyes – 'I tried it once or twice.'

Again he felt convinced that this was only part of the truth. She knew more than she was willing to tell.

He said, 'I've always thought of Robert and you as the ideal married couple who had no secrets from each other.'

A shadow of grief settled on her face. She wrapped both

arms round herself and bit on her lower lip while she stared at nothing for a long time.

At last, she said, 'That's how we used to be. But people change. Not that I'm blaming him. When these things happen it's never one-sided. I'm – I'm equally to blame.'

'Did you quarrel a lot?'

'No, I wouldn't exactly call it that. Mostly petty bickering.'

'That's what destroys a marriage more surely than anything else,' Piper said. 'An honest straightforward row often clears the air.'

'Yes, I suppose so.' She seemed glad he had turned a shapeless admission into something concrete. 'Robert and I haven't had a really frank talk in ages.'

'How did you come to drift apart?'

Lynn was less than happy at the question. She looked down at her restless hands while she tried to think of an answer.

Then she shrugged. She said, 'I can't even remember how it all began. Grew out of nothing, really. At the beginning I put it down to overwork. Now I realize I might've been a little more understanding . . .'

'If it wasn't overwork, what was it?'

Once again she needed time to think. When she forced herself to look up, she said, 'I lay awake last night, hour after hour, trying to find a reason for what happened on Saturday but there wasn't one. With any other man, maybe. But not with Robert.'

The look of pain in her eyes betrayed an almost physical suffering. Piper could guess what she meant. It brought back something Quinn had asked.

'. . . *Would you say he's been a faithful husband?*'

And later there had been a remark along the same lines :
'. . . *I think there's a woman in this affair.*'

Piper said, 'With anyone but Robert you'd have suspectd that the trouble might be some other woman.'

Lynn Heseltine nodded, her pretty mouth drawn in. Only

just above a whisper, she murmured, 'Even now, I can't make myself believe it. The very idea is absurd.'

'When you say even now, does that mean you have some evidence that other people might accept?'

'Not – ' she shook her head – 'not what I'd call evidence.'

Something in her face told Piper she could be persuaded to believe it, that the alternative was even more distasteful. Perhaps that was what lay behind her confession that she was equally to blame. Perhaps they had not been husband and wife in the fullest sense. If that were so, Robert Heseltine might well have turned to some other woman.

'I can't help unless you're frank with me,' Piper said. 'Have you any reason at all to suspect that Robert has been unfaithful?'

'No, but – ' She stumbled over the next word and began again. 'Reason seldom has anything to do with it. When things go wrong between two people both of them share the responsibility. If he needed someone else it must've been because I failed him.'

'That's all very well. But it doesn't explain why he should want to commit suicide. At the very worst, all you could do was divorce him.'

She gave Piper a little twisted smile. She said, 'I wouldn't have done that. He meant too much to me.'

'Are you saying you'd have gone on living with him even after you had proof that he'd got a mistress?'

'No, he'd have had to give her up. Then we could've tried to make a fresh start.'

'You're an unusual woman,' Piper said.

'Don't flatter me.' The look of pain was back in her eyes. 'This is all talk. If Robert is dead we'll never know if I'd have gone through with it.'

'Perhaps not. But the whole question is why he should be dead. He had no motive for taking his own life. An unfaithful husband doesn't commit suicide. I've never heard of one who did.'

Lynn Heseltine lowered her arms in a helpless gesture. She moistened her lips and said, 'You don't understand . . . and I can't explain.'

'Why not?'

'Because I don't want anything to harm his good name . . . if he gave his life to preserve it. He might even have felt he was protecting me from being hurt, as well.'

'A man isn't ostracised because he commits misconduct,' Piper said. 'Those days are long past. To suggest —'

There Piper stopped. What he saw in her eyes left him no room to argue.

She went on looking at him in silence. He felt she was relieved that he had stumbled on the truth without having to be told.

Now so many things had become clear. He asked, 'Was this woman one of Robert's patients?'

Lynn moistened her lips again. She said, 'I'm not going to say any more unless you promise you won't tell anybody. It could be just sheer nonsense and I'd be creating a scandal without any justification.'

Piper said, 'You have my promise. Whatever you tell me will be strictly confidential . . . providing I'm not questioned by the police.'

'Why should they question you?'

'No reason that I can think of. But since they're investigating Robert's disappearance, it's just faintly possible.'

That seemed to satisfy her. He had an uneasy feeling that she had wanted all along to confide in him. Why it should make him feel uneasy was just part of the atmosphere in this quiet melancholy house.

Her hands twined and untwined nervously before at last she said, 'It never entered my mind that there could be another woman . . . until this morning. I don't want to believe it even now. It's absolutely crazy to imagine . . .'

'What happened this morning?'

'A letter arrived. It was addressed to Robert . . .' She

swallowed as though something had caught in her throat.

'In the circumstances you were entitled to open it,' Piper said.

'Yes . . . but we've never opened each other's mail.'

In a dull voice, she added, 'I felt I was being mean.' Her tired eyes were asking for further reassurance.

'That would only apply if you were snooping,' Piper said. 'What was in the letter?'

'A lot of wild talk. I still don't believe Robert could've had anything to do with a woman like that. At first I was tempted to phone her but then I had second thoughts. It might do more harm than good to let her think I was taking her seriously.'

'Who is this woman?'

'Her name's Gordon – Pauline Gordon.'

'Have you ever met her?'

'No, but – ' Mrs Heseltine looked away – 'we had a short conversation on the phone Saturday morning. She wanted to speak to Robert.'

'What about?'

'Didn't say. Just mentioned that she was one of his patients. I advised her to ring the Clinic.'

'When was this phone call?'

'About midday.'

'Did she indulge in any wild talk on the phone?'

'No, rather subdued . . . if anything. I got the impression she was a bit upset but I didn't ask any questions. I never have had much to do with his patients.'

Piper separated one detail from what he remembered of the events of Saturday morning. He asked, 'When Robert phoned you to say he'd been detained and wouldn't be leaving for Dorchester until the evening, did you tell him this Pauline Gordon had rung here?'

'No, I didn't think of it.'

'So you can't say whether or not she spoke to him at the hospital?'

After a short pause, Lynn Heseltine said, 'No.' That hurt

look was in her eyes again. 'Robert's secretary would know
... but I'd rather you didn't discuss it with her. What difference can it make?'

'Maybe more than you think,' Piper said. 'I'll be better
able to tell you when I've seen the letter you received this
morning. You've still got it, I hope?'

'Yes, it's upstairs. I didn't want to leave it lying around
. . .'

She hesitated. Then she went out hastily as though afraid
she might change her mind.

When she had gone he got out of his chair and walked to
and fro in an effort to rid himself of his mounting uneasi-
ness. Lynn might have been telling the truth but it was not
the whole truth. Behind her admissions there was a secret
within a secret.

No one as beautiful and charming as Lynn Heseltine
should ever have lost her husband to another woman. Men
often did foolish things. Temptation could catch a man off
guard – even a man whose training and discipline had
taught him self-control. But Robert would not merely have
risked sacrificing his marriage : the price of misconduct was
the destruction of his professional career.

. . . *He would've had to be mad to chance throwing away
everything he represented, everything he'd worked for. If
it is true, then this Pauline Gordon must be something
special. Whether Lynn agrees or not, I've got to see what
kind of woman could make him give up the good life for
her sake . . .*

That was what it had meant in the end. Robert Heseltine had given up his life. And the motive now seemed only
too clear.

There had come a time when Heseltine's infatuation had
burned itself out. He had wanted to be free . . . and Pauline
Gordon had refused to give him his freedom. For her it was
not over. If he tried to break off their relationship she
would expose him.

And the consequences were more than Robert Heseltine

could face. She had phoned him at the hospital on Saturday morning and delivered her ultimatum. On his way to Dorchester he had recognized the inevitable. Only one course lay open to him. There was no escape.

However many times Piper shifted the pieces around they always formed the same pattern. Those last three hours of Heseltine's life had ceased to be a problem. Pauline Gordon was the answer.

Quinn had been right, as he was so often right. '. . . *I think there's a woman in this affair.*'

Yet . . . Piper was still disturbed by a lingering doubt. Something was incomplete, something just out of sight was missing.

It all seemed just too simple. Among other things it ignored his instinct that Lynn Heseltine was afraid. Whether her fear was the outcome of guilt or a sense of impending evil might be the key to what had happened on Saturday evening between seven o'clock and a quarter to ten . . .

Through the half-open door he saw Lynn coming down the stairs. She was very beautiful but it was a pale remote beauty without any life. Even the hint of some inner fear had gone.

She came in and handed him an envelope with a torn flap. She said, 'It arrived by the first post.'

It was franked Aug. 20 and time-stamped 1.45 p.m. The addresss was in flowing script and the same hand had written diagonally in the top left-hand corner : *PRIVATE.*

As he opened the folded letter, Mrs Heseltine walked to the window and stood with her back turned. He guessed that she had no wish to let him see the look on her face while he read what some other woman had written to her husband.

The notepaper had a die-stamped address : 56 Northwood Avenue, West Brompton, London SW10. It was cheap paper in a pale blue that matched the envelope.

There was no date, nothing to show when the letter had been written. And it began without any salutation.

You may be able to forget what we have been to each other but I cannot deny the love I have for you. It means more to me than life itself. Now the time has come when you must choose between your wife and me. If you think I can be thrown aside because you have had your fun you are very much mistaken.

As a man of honour there is only one decision you can make. I do not have to tell you what people would say if they knew how you had behaved.

But public opinion is unimportant. You know that I cannot live without you. Whatever the future may hold I promise you that my love will not be found wanting.

Pauline.

Lynn Heseltine was still looking out of the window when Piper read the letter a second time. Then he asked, 'What sort of person could write like this? Do you believe the things she says?'

With her eyes on the sunlit garden, Lynn said, 'I've already told you I don't know what to believe.'

'Did she sound queer when she spoke to you on the phone?'

'No, just rather – well, rather nervous.'

'This isn't what I'd have expected from somebody who was nervous. It's high-flown and melodramatic . . . like the language you'd find in an old-fashioned novelette.'

'That doesn't interest me.' Lynn swung round, her lips trembling. 'The letter says enough to make the situation plain. If this woman Gordon rang the hospital after speaking to me and if she used the same kind of threats . . .'

'You think Robert could have been driven to take his own life,' Piper said.

'Yes.'

As though her emotions had been bottled up too long, Lynn repeated fiercely, 'Yes . . . yes . . . yes!' Then she covered her face with both hands and went very still.

'You may be right,' Piper said. 'But I'm not yet con-

vinced. If you don't mind I'd like to call on Pauline Gordon
and ask her if she did talk to Robert on Saturday.'

Through her fingers, Lynn said, 'I can't stop you . . .
and I don't suppose it'll do him any harm. But protect him
as much as you can.'

'Of course. May I keep this letter for the time being?'

'If you wish.' She lowered her hands and looked up, dry-
eyed and miserable. 'I never want to see it again.'

He left her standing lonely and forlorn with sunshine all
around her like an illuminated figure of grief. The picture
of her ravaged face stayed in his mind as he walked down
the drive and through the big double gates.

Perhaps Robert Heseltine had made a fool of himself
with a woman patient. Perhaps there was no mystery in
what had happened on Saturday evening between seven
o'clock and a quarter to ten. Perhaps the explanation was
in that prosy letter.

If it were, then Pauline Gordon would know. And it
should not be very difficult to make Pauline Gordon tell
what she knew.

CHAPTER VI

NORTHWOOD AVENUE was off the Fulham Road, not more
than five minutes by car from the Brompton Clinic. Dwarf
trees lined the pavements at twenty-yard intervals and
there were trim grass borders outside each semi-detached
house.

Number 56 looked little different from its neighbours:
low boundary wall between pavement and garden, minia-
ture lawn, tarmac path, eighteen-inch high lattice fence
separating it from the path belonging to number 58. One
house was painted white, the other light green. That seemed
the main difference.

As Piper got out of his car he noticed that the net curtains in number 56 were not as spruce as those on either
side. In the late afternoon sun he also saw that the window
frames and the doorway needed repainting. Compared with
its neighbours, Pauline Gordon's house had an air of
neglect.

He tried the bell-push but the button was stuck. So he
used his knuckles on the leaded-glass panel above the letter
box.

There was no reply. When he knocked again with the
same result he told himself his visit might prove to have
been a waste of time.

. . . *Saved me a lot of trouble if she was on the phone.*
Maybe, of course, I'd have preferred not to warn her I was
calling. Can't have it both ways . . .

Another rat-tat on the glass panel convinced him there
was no one at home. Then as he was turning away he
thought he could hear faint sounds inside the house. They
were so far away they might have come from somewhere
else.

He went round to the back door and looked in through a

window at what appeared to be the kitchen. The place was empty. A bottle of milk stood on the doorstep.

When he returned to the front porch he caught sight of something he had overlooked before. The flap of the letter-box was jammed partly open. When he stooped and looked closer he could see the protruding end of a rolled-up news-paper.

By standing against the door he was able to hear the distant sound of what could have been a child wailing. A moment later it faded away and the house was silent again.

He knocked once more – louder this time. As he listened intently the wailing noise returned. Now it sounded less like a fretful child than he had at first thought.

Even if it were . . . Nobody had the right to leave a child alone for any length of time.

Two separate thoughts suddenly coalesced in his mind: the bottle of milk that had not been taken in and the folded newspaper still in the letter-box. One might have been forgotten but surely not both.

. . . Unless somebody went out in a hurry . . . or before the paper and the milk were delivered. In either case, who-ever's making that noise is alone . . . and may have been alone for many hours . . .

Piper's next thought painted an even grimmer picture. Those lonely hours could well have begun the previous day. It all depended on what time the milkman had called at number 56.

If nobody had heard that thin wailing voice when it started to complain there would have been little chance of hearing it now. Only chance had brought him here. But for that, it could have been Tuesday morning before anyone noticed the untouched bottle of milk on the back door-step.

He listened for a moment longer. Then he crossed the path and stepped over the low lattice fence separating num-ber 56 from number 58.

A woman answered the door – a stout, bright-eyed

woman wearing carpet slippers. She had a double set of dentures that seemed too large for her mouth.

She asked, 'Yes?'

Piper said, 'Sorry to trouble you . . . but I wanted to speak to your neighbour, Miss Gordon, and I can't get any reply although I think there's somebody at home. Have you seen her today?'

'No, I haven't.' The bright-eyed woman smiled aimlessly. 'You'll have heard her mother, I expect.'

'Well, she didn't seem to hear me. I knocked repeatedly but there was no answer.'

'Ah, that's because she's not very good on her feet. Got arthritis and can't move around much . . . poor dear. Takes her a while to get to the door.'

'I waited quite a while,' Piper said. 'All I could hear was a peculiar sound like somebody in pain. Is it possible Mrs Gordon has been taken ill?'

The stout woman sucked at her dentures. Then she said, 'I wouldn't know, I'm sure. The old lady seemed all right last time I spoke to her.'

'When was that?'

'Saturday morning. She was taking in the milk and we passed the time of day.'

'She hasn't taken in the milk this morning. Do they get any on a Sunday?'

'No, the milkman doesn't call.'

With a growing look of concern, the stout woman added, 'Hope nothing's wrong. Could it have been the radio you heard? Might've deceived you into thinking –'

'It wasn't the radio,' Piper said. 'It was the kind of crying noise a child makes. Very faint . . . but I couldn't be mistaken.'

'Oh, I see. Well, there are no children in the house . . . that I can tell you. Just Miss Gordon and her mother.'

There an even sharper look came into the stout woman's eyes. She said, 'Funny, when you come to think of it . . .'

'What is?'

'Miss Gordon should be at home. She's a cashier at Quality Stores, the supermarket, and they're closed on a Monday.'

'Could she have gone out shopping?'

'It's possible . . . but not if her mother's ill.'

Piper glanced over his shoulder at number 56. He said, 'Perhaps she's gone to phone for the doctor.'

The stout woman's air of concern evaporated. She said, 'Ah, yes, that's what it must be. She should be back soon.'

'Where's the nearest phone box?'

'Top of the avenue. Only a few minutes' walk.'

'Then I'd better wait,' Piper said.

He stepped over the dividing trellis and listened again at the door of number 56. The stout woman stood watching him, one hand shielding her eyes from the sun.

Inside Pauline Gordon's house someone was still making plaintive sounds that he now thought came from an upstairs room. On the ground floor everything was quiet.

Soon the wailing died away. When it began again it was much fainter – just a distant crying voice that was infinitely pathetic.

The minutes passed. Piper saw the next-door neighbour walk down to her gate and stare in both directions along Northwood Avenue.

When she turned to look at him, she called out, 'No sign of Miss Gordon yet. Can't imagine where she could've got to.'

There was now complete silence in number 56. Piper said, 'She's had time to get to the phone box and back again twice over. We ought to do something.'

The stout woman returned to her own doorway. In a worried voice, she said, 'What can we do? I don't fancy poking my nose into other people's affairs.'

A phrase from the letter Lynn Heseltine had shown him repeated itself in Piper's mind. Now it had a new significance.

He said, 'I can't just walk away and ignore the possibility that Mrs Gordon is ill and alone in the house. It's immaterial where her daughter has gone.'

'That's as may be. What d'you suggest?'

'Our best plan would be to get in touch with the police. They'll know what action to take.'

'The police? That's a bit much, isn't it?'

'No, I don't think so.' Faint and far away he could once more hear the thin wailing of somebody in pain. 'If Miss Gordon should come back while I'm at the phone box you can tell her where I've gone.'

'All right.' A look of greedy fascination sharpened the neighbour's bright little eyes. 'Nothing like this has ever happened before. They're quiet-living people who keep to themselves. Miss Gordon seldom goes out after she gets home from work. Beats me where she can be on a Monday.'

'I wouldn't even try to guess,' Piper said.

There were two girls in the phone box at the end of Northwood Avenue. While he was trying to decide what he should do he caught sight of a police patrol car cruising slowly towards him.

When Piper flagged it down it pulled into the kerb and the driver got out. He was a bulky fresh-complexioned sergeant with ginger hair.

He asked, 'Can I help you, sir?'

'I'd be glad of your advice,' Piper said. 'I've reason to believe somebody is ill at number 56 where people called Gordon live. Whether it's serious or not is impossible to say because her daughter is out . . .'

The ginger sergeant listened, his eyes on Piper's face. Then he said, 'If you'll drive back to the house, sir, I'll follow behind you.'

Outside number 58 the stout woman and a wizened little man with a shopping bag were talking together. She was still wearing her slippers.

Their conversation broke off as the two cars pulled up at the house next door. Across the street a girl pushing a pram stopped to see what was going on.

When they reached the porch, the uniformed sergeant said, 'Let's see if I get any answer.'

He beat his knuckles on the leaded-glass panel several times, then stooped and put his ear to the flap of the letter-box. After a few seconds he looked up at Piper and asked, 'Is that what you heard, sir?'

Piper said, 'Yes. What does it sound like to you?'

'I'm inclined to agree somebody must be ill and needs help. If you don't mind waiting here, sir . . .'

He walked round the side of the house and took out his pocket radio transmitter. With his back to Piper he spoke in a lowered voice.

'. . . Yes, I think so . . . shouldn't be difficult . . . can't say how long the old lady's been on her own . . . very well . . . I'll call in when I've found out the score . . .'

In an upstairs room the thin frail voice was moaning again as he came back into the porch. He said, 'Right, sir. I've been given the go-ahead. You'd better keep out of the way.'

It was a swift, efficient operation. He balanced himself on one leg, raised his other foot at right-angles to his body and smashed it against the key-hole with tremendous force. There was a report like a gunshot as the lock yielded and the door whipped open.

With barely a pause, the sergeant went inside. Over his shoulder, he said, 'I'd like you to come with me, sir. And please shut the door or we'll be giving half the street free entertainment.'

Piper followed him upstairs. When they reached the landing they could see into bathroom and toilet. Two other doors were shut. The last one was open just enough to reveal a wardrobe and the foot of a bed.

It was in there that someone was moaning with the regularity of each laboured breath. Piper felt his skin prickle as the sergeant went inside. Something made him almost afraid to look. He could feel all around him an atmosphere of pain and utter despair.

Then the door was open wide and the atmosphere became reality. On the floor beside the bed lay a haggard old woman in a nightdress. One arm was outstretched past her head, the other was drawn in close to her motionless body.

More than anything else it was the look of suffering on her gaunt face that roused all Piper's compassion. A strand of tangled grey hair covered one eye. The other had a vacant stare as though her sight had gone.

Only her lips retained some measure of life – thin bloodless lips that twitched with every shallow breath. As the sergeant bent over her, she clawed weakly at the carpet and groaned '. . . Help me . . . please, somebody help me . . .'

He said, 'Poor old biddy. Wonder how long she's been lying here like this?'

'I'd say since yesterday at the very least,' Piper said. 'She's barely conscious. Looks as if she fell getting out of bed and injured herself. Probably got a broken bone.'

'To be on the safe side we'll not move her. But I don't suppose a drop of water can do any harm. Would you get some from the bathroom, sir, while I try to make her comfortable?'

The tumbler on a shelf above the wash-basin had been used as a toothbrush holder. While he was rinsing it thoroughly, Piper could hear the sergeant talking to the local station on his transmitter.

Apart from his soft voice and the scratchy response asking a question or two, there was no other sound in the house. The old woman was no longer moaning. Piper wondered if deliverance might not have come too late.

She was still breathing in little shallow breaths when he went back into the bedroom. The sergeant had put a pillow under her head and covered her with the quilt but he had not disturbed the position in which she lay.

He said, 'Hope the ambulance gets here soon. She looks pretty far gone, to me. If you'll give me that tumbler, sir . . .'

Very carefully he tipped some water into her open mouth. Most of it ran out but her lips closed on the remaining few drops. She swallowed and groaned and her breathing deepened.

The sergeant said, 'Don't think I'll risk letting her have more. We've done all we can. Good job you arrived when you did, sir.'

It was an implied question. Piper said, 'I wanted to talk to her daughter. Looks as if she went somewhere and was prevented from coming back. Wouldn't have abandoned her mother like this from choice.'

'Perhaps the old lady was all right when Miss Gordon left.

'Yes, but that must've been some considerable time ago or her mother wouldn't be in this state. My opinion is that she's been lying here at least twenty-four hours . . . probably a lot longer.'

'Which means daughter didn't come home last night.'

'Or possibly even the night before.'

'Doesn't bear thinking about.' The ginger-haired sergeant looked down at the old woman and shook his head. 'Poor old biddy. If her daughter went off just like that, they must've had a row. Don't know how she could do it.'

Piper said, 'Taking care of an elderly person can tax anybody's patience.'

'Maybe so. But I'll bet she won't feel so happy when she gets back and hears what happened to her mother.'

'If she intends to come back. She may have packed up and left for good. Mrs Gordon might even have told her to get out.'

'Soon regretted it – ' the sergeant glanced down at the old woman again – 'if she did. However, we'll have to wait and see.'

A phrase from Pauline's letter kept insinuating itself in Piper's thoughts : '. . . *Whatever the future may hold I promise you my love will not be found wanting.*'

Anyone who could write like that was likely to do something extravagant under stress. Perhaps they had quarrelled because Mrs Gordon found out her daughter was having an affaire. Perhaps Pauline had stated bluntly that it was her own life and she intended to live it as she pleased. She was no longer prepared to act as breadwinner – companion – nurse – housekeeper.

That could have been what she had told Heseltine . . . if she had phoned him on Saturday. And the knowledge that she had abandoned her mother because of him was the last straw.

There were bound to be some indications if she had left home. No law stopped Piper taking a look to satisfy his curiosity while he had the chance.

He said, 'I'll put this glass back in the bathroom. You won't want it again, will you?'

The sergeant bent over Mrs Gordon and began feeling for the pulse in her outstretched arm. Without looking up he shook his head.

It took Piper only seconds to stand the tumbler on the glass shelf. Then he came out on to the landing and opened the nearer door very quietly.

The room had no real furniture. In the centre lay a worn carpet square surrounded by bare floorboards. There were partly-drawn curtains over the window, three or four suit-cases in one corner and a wooden chest behind the door. On the chest stood a mattress inadequately protected by a wrapping of brown paper tied with string.

He backed out and closed the door without a sound. As he turned the knob of the adjoining door he heard Mrs Gordon mumble a few words like somebody talking in her sleep.

Slowly and cautiously he eased the door open and went inside. He knew he would not have long. The ambulance would be arriving any minute. He had to be quick if he wanted to satisfy his theory about Pauline Gordon.

This room was furnished. It had a single bed, a wardrobe, a dressing-table and a chest of drawers. All of it was cheap.

All of it was far from new.

The carpet and the lino surrounds had also had plenty of wear. In the light from the window he could see a worn patch alongside the bed and another in front of the dressing table.

But these were not the things that halted him before he had taken a second step. Now he realized how it was that old Mrs Gordon had lain so long broken and despairing on the floor of her room. Now he knew why she could have gone on wailing for help that never came if chance had not brought him to number 56 Northwood Avenue.

There was a woman lying on the bed – a fair-haired woman with the features of a pretty doll. She was fully dressed except for her shoes. Her eyes were shut and her face had no more life than the face of a doll sleeping in make-believe.

One thing above all else told Piper that this was a sleep from which she would never waken. Where he stood he could see her left wrist and the deep gash that had severed the arteries.

Blood had spurted all around her and on to the floor. Under her arm a reddish-brown mess of congealed blood had soaked into the bedspread. In her right hand she was loosely holding a knife with a short pointed blade.

The nausea churning inside him welled up into his throat. He backed out on to the landing and swallowed several times until the feeling of sickness passed.

As he was recovering his breath he heard the jangle of an ambulance bell coming rapidly nearer. It roused him to a sudden awareness of what lay ahead.

He called out, 'Sergeant! You'd better come and take a look in the next room . . .'

CHAPTER VII

OLD MRS GORDON was still alive when she was carried out of the house. A second ambulance took her daughter to the mortuary.

By then a police photographer had taken a series of pictures and the fingerprint man had finished his work. When they drove off, the cluster of sightseeing neighbours on the pavement dispersed. Only Piper's car and a police vehicle with a uniformed driver remained outside number 56 Northwood Avenue.

After the coming and going of many busy people the house was very quiet. Detective-Inspector Cattanoch said they were likely to get more peace there than at the local station.

'. . . The back room downstairs will do nicely. It's not over-furnished but we only need a couple of chairs.'

He was a tall lean man with thinning hair and a colourless face. His eyes were watchful, his manner restrained.

With his hands in his coat pockets he paced from door to window and back to the middle of the room again. Then he spread his feet apart, put both hands behind him and rocked up and down.

After a long silence, he said, 'I know you by reputation, Mr Piper. From what I've heard I can rely on your co-operation in my inquiries.'

'To the best of my ability,' Piper said.

'That's good enough for me. Suppose you start off by explaining how you came to be here.'

'I wanted to have a talk with Pauline Gordon.'

'Have you met her before?'

'No, I never heard of her until this afternoon when I visited the home of some friends of mine – the Heseltines of Canon's Park. You probably read about Mr Heseltine in today's paper.'

Disclosure was inevitable. Piper had known that ever since he found Pauline Gordon's body. Any endeavour to conceal what lay behind her death would serve no purpose at all. He could not protect Robert Heseltine . . . and beyond any doubt he would make serious trouble for himself if he even tried.

The truth was bound to come out. Whatever he had promised Lynn there was now no way he could shield her . . .

Nothing changed in Cattanoch's spare face. He asked, 'Do you mean the London surgeon whose car was found abandoned somewhere on the South Coast?'

'Yes.'

'What connection is there between Mr Heseltine and this Pauline Gordon?'

'She was one of his patients.'

'And?'

'This morning his wife received a letter that Miss Gordon had written to him,' Piper said. 'It was a strange communication . . . especially in the light of what happened on Saturday.'

'Have you got this letter?'

'Yes. Mrs Heseltine allowed me to keep it.'

'Good. Do you mind letting me see it?'

'Not at all . . .'

Inspector Cattanoch read the letter and stood bobbing his head reflectively. Then he asked, 'Would you say this thing can be taken at its face value?'

Piper said, 'Not from my knowledge of Robert Heseltine. Until I've heard his side of the story I wouldn't jump to conclusions.'

'What if you didn't get the chance to hear his side?'

'I'd still reserve judgment.'

'You're a loyal friend,' Cattanoch said.

It sounded like an innocent comment but Piper felt there was just a hint of a warning behind it. He said, 'Not necessarily. You forget we're talking about a professional man of very high repute.'

'Perhaps so.' The inspector allowed himself a momentary smile. 'In my job one tends to ignore the advice of the three wise monkeys.'

He put the letter back in its envelope and added, 'However, judging by Miss Gordon's remarks she's been more than merely a patient of Mr Heseltine.'

'There's no proof of that yet,' Piper said. 'Women in her circumstances have been known to create phantasies. Attachment to a doctor isn't uncommon. The fact that she took her own life indicates some degree of mental unbalance'.

'Indications aren't evidence. We've no proof of anything yet.'

'I'm not sure –' Piper had a picture in his mind of Pauline's bloodless face – 'that I understand what you mean.'

Cattanoch rocked to and fro a couple of times. He said, 'I was merely taking a leaf out of your book. Didn't you advise against jumping to conclusions?'

'Yes . . . but you're using it in connection with something different.'

'Very true. I say you're jumping to conclusions when you state it's a fact that she took her own life.'

Once again Piper was standing in the doorway of the room that reeked of death. What he had discovered was horror enough. This suggestion went too far.

He said, 'Are you seriously asking me to believe that Robert Heseltine could've had anything to do with it?'

'But of course he did. Directly or indirectly, innocently or otherwise, Heseltine motivated what happened.'

'That's not the same thing. You're suggesting that it might not have been suicide.'

In a calm precise voice, Cattanoch said, 'Not quite. What I questioned was your statement that it was a fact. From what you've told me there are only two established facts in this case: Pauline Gordon is dead and Robert Heseltine has disappeared.'

Piper had an uncomfortable feeling he was being led along the road that Cattanoch wanted him to follow. Heseltine had been charged and found guilty without the opportunity of speaking in his own defence. It would not be long before he became enmeshed in a web from which he would never escape.

If he were still alive . . . Piper said, 'That doesn't mean she didn't take her own life.'

'There I wouldn't argue. But the time factor may be against it. Of course, it might well have been a coincidence.'

'What might?'

'Pauline Gordon is believed to have died on Saturday afternoon,' Cattanoch said.

So many of Piper's questions had now been answered all at once. So many pieces now fell into place. The Brompton Clinic was only a few minutes' journey by car to Northwood Avenue. If Pauline had phoned the hospital and repeated the threats contained in her letter. Heseltine could have visited number 56 in an attempt to reason with her. When he called, old Mrs Gordon might have been taking her after-lunch sleep . . .

Piper said, 'According to what I've been told, Heseltine was at the hospital all Saturday afternoon. He had to perform an urgent operation and didn't set off for Dorchester until nearly seven o'clock in the evening.'

'I see.' Cattanoch nodded thoughtfully. 'Would you mind telling me what else you've been told about his movements that day?'

'No, of course I don't mind. But I still think you're barking up the wrong tree.'

'That's putting it too strongly. All I'm asking for is information.'

'Well, I'll give you everything I've learned since I read the paragraph about Heseltine in the *Morning Post*,' Piper said.

The inspector listened without interruption, his hands in his pockets, his face impassive. When he had heard it all he still remained distantly reflective.

At last, he said, 'We've a long way to go . . . but maybe it's the right tree. No proof yet, of course.'

'You'll need cast-iron proof to convince me,' Piper said. 'I just won't believe she was murdered by Robert Heseltine . . . assuming she was murdered.'

'As a supposition – ' Cattanoch thrust his hands deeper in his pockets – 'it's worth pursuing. And if we find it stands up, then Heseltine is a logical suspect.'

'Only because you don't know the man.'

'Perhaps so. But I know more important things. The threat in her letter provides the motive. The estimated time of death fits the time he was understood to have gone somewhere for lunch . . . so he had the opportunity.'

With a shrug, Cattanoch added, 'The means can be bought in any general store.'

'You seem to have it all cut and dried.'

'Not really. I'm merely trying it out on the dog . . . if you'll forgive the expression. May I take you into my confidence, Mr Piper?'

'Of course. I won't broadcast anything you say to me.'

'Well, it's like this. The police surgeon found traces of what appears to be saliva on the pillow. That could mean it was held over her face to stop her making a row . . . couldn't it?'

'Only if the person who killed her had three hands,' Piper said. 'One to hold down the pillow, another to grip her left wrist, a third hand to use the knife.'

'Not if he lay across the pillow while he was doing it and then held her helpless until she became too weak to struggle.'

'I should imagine she'd have suffocated by that time.'

'Wouldn't take long,' Cattanoch said. 'A deep gash of that nature results in a rapid loss of blood. She'd become unconscious very quickly. Soon as she passed out, somebody whose name we won't mention replaced the pillow under her head, wiped his fingerprints off the knife and put it in her hand. When you've thought about it you'll have to agree it could well have happened that way.'

Piper said, 'I've thought about it and I don't agree. All the circumstances could just as easily apply to suicide.'

'Except that severing one's wrist isn't pleasant. Much simpler to take an overdose of sleeping pills . . . and we found a container half full of them in one of the dressing-table drawers.'

'Still doesn't prove anything. Suicide isn't considered to be a rational act.'

'Exactly.' Cattanoch looked momentarily smug. 'That's where it differs from murder. However, all I've got right now is a theory.'

'And a wild one, at that.'

'You could be right. All the same, it would account for Heseltine's disappearance. Guilt . . . remorse . . . who knows how a man feels when he's killed his mistress?'

Piper said, 'Not a man like Robert Heseltine. It's just too absurd.'

'If he's still alive you may change your mind. It means he deliberately planned to disappear and the letter written by Miss Gordon explains why.'

'I don't see that. Once she was dead he had nothing to fear. The threat of exposure had been eliminated. He didn't know, perhaps, that she'd write but it made no difference anyway. He'd have received the letter himself and so nobody else would ever have seen it.'

After a long thoughtful silence, Cattanach said, 'Good thinking, Mr Piper, very good thinking. You certainly live up to your reputation. Fortunately this discussion has been strictly between ourselves.'

He jingled some loose change in his pocket. Then he added, 'If your friend Heseltine has gone for good we'll never know what really happened, I'm afraid.'

'It's only Heseltine I'm worried about,' Piper said. 'The

reason for Miss Gordon's death is quite academic. As I see it, she had one of two motives for committing suicide: either she'd been having an affaire with Heseltine and he broke it off or she created a phantasy around him and couldn't bear to face reality when he showed her the truth.'

'Either way –' the inspector drew down his long face in a frown – 'there remains a problem which I'm glad isn't mine. What did Heseltine do after he abandoned his car on the cliffs last Saturday night?'

Piper remembered the look of misery in Lynn's eyes when he left her standing like a figure of grief in the little room looking out on a sunlit garden. She thought she knew where her husband had gone and she had no hope of ever seeing him again.

In the recesses of his mind he could hear her uneven voice. '. . . *If he needed someone else it must've been because I failed him.*'

Why she had made that admission was her own secret. If Piper was any judge it was a secret compounded of some inner guilt.

'. . . *When these things happen it's never one-sided. I'm equally to blame.*'

A sudden realization grew to monstrous size in his thoughts. Now two people were talking.

'. . . *At the very worst all you could do was divorce him.*'

'*I wouldn't have done that. He meant too much to me . . .*'

If Lynn had known there was another woman. If Lynn had known . . . That could explain the look of guilt in her eyes. But it provided no explanation for her husband's disappearance.

Inspector Cattanoch was saying '. . . I must get back to the station and make out my report. You know you'll be called to give evidence at the inquest, of course?'

Piper said, 'Yes. Will that letter have to be produced?'

'At this stage I couldn't say. The proceedings may be adjourned and a lot depends on what happens after that.'

'So I would imagine. Give me a ring if I'm needed in the meantime.'

There was a tentative knock at the door. A man in overalls poked his head in and asked, 'Will it trouble you if I start repairing that lock?'

'It's got to be done,' Cattanoch said. 'How long will it take?'

'Half an hour or thereabouts.'

'Then I'll send an officer to lock up when you've finished. Let nobody in – nobody at all.'

'Right. I'll see to it . . .'

Cattanoch and Piper went outside. As they walked to the gate, Piper said, 'If you still doubt that it was suicide, I suggest you fit Miss Gordon's letter into your time-table of events, beginning with the doctor's estimate of the time of death.'

'How does it fit in your reckoning?'

'Well, if she rang Heseltine at the hospital on Saturday, it would be reasonable to assume that their conversation on the phone inspired what she put in her letter. You agree?'

'Yes. Go on.'

'What if she didn't phone him?'

'But the odds are she did. We know she tried to get him at his home.'

'That was different. I've an idea she didn't try again. There's no mention in her letter of any conversation and so I think she went back home and wrote to him.'

'Your theories are as vague as mine,' Cattanoch said. 'I see no reason why she couldn't have spoken to him.'

'One thing's against it. Mrs Heseltine says she received the call about midday. That being so, Pauline Gordon had roughly three-quarters of an hour to return home from the phone box, write her letter and take it out to post. Doesn't leave much time to have a talk with Heseltine. For a start, the hospital switchboard would've had to find him. He wouldn't be immediately available if he were visiting one of the wards . . . would he?'

Inspector Cattanoch unlatched the gate and opened it before he said, 'You're going too fast for me. Why do you say she had only three-quarters of an hour?'

'Because the envelope is time-stamped 1.45 p.m. I had a query with the post office some months ago and I learned that you have to allow an hour between collection and franking. That means her letter couldn't have been posted any later than 12.45 p.m. Now do you see?'

'To some extent – yes. I must admit you have a point. But I'd like confirmation that she didn't speak to Heseltine.'

'You might never get it. All depends on someone remembering if there was such a call. If they don't – '

'We'll have no proof either way,' Cattanoch said. 'Unless, of course . . .'

He hesitated only for a moment. Then his eyes brightened and he asked, 'Have you thought that the letter might've been written before she went out to the phone box to ring Heseltine's home number?'

'No. And it doesn't seem very likely to me.'

'Lots of things have happened in the past couple of days – ' Inspector Cattanoch gave Piper a parting nod – 'that wouldn't have seemed very likely before they happened. Let me know if you have any new ideas. I've enjoyed our little chat . . .'

CHAPTER VIII

WHEN PIPER GOT BACK to his office he made three phone calls. The first one told him nothing he had not expected.

Old Mrs Gordon was out of immediate danger but she had not yet recovered sufficiently to be rational. The ward sister said the old woman had a strong constitution but it would take time.

'. . . At her age a fractured femur presents obvious difficulties. She was considerably dehydrated, as well. Taken all round she won't be fit to have visitors for several days, at the very least . . . assuming she continues to make progress.'

'I'll phone again tomorrow,' Piper said.

The need to make his second call worried him. If he had not visited Lynn Heseltine he would never have known about that damning letter. Miss Gordon's death would have been treated as a case of suicide . . . and there would now be nothing to connect her with the disappearance of Robert Heseltine.

For his wife the scandal had been bad enough. Now she had to carry a greater weight of publicity when his name was dragged through the gutter.

And all this could have been avoided. The pity was that she had ever disclosed the existence of that damn letter. Time and again Piper kept telling himself he should have minded his own business.

Yet . . . If he were a fatalist he would see himself as an instrument of Providence. His visit to Lynn Heseltine had led him to the house in Northwood Avenue in time to save an old woman's life.

Perhaps there was a pattern in these things. Jane always thought so. She believed some people died that others might

live. As a philosophy it seemed to lack justice . . . especially
in this case.

The innocent suffered with the guilty. But appearances
could be deceptive. Lyn confessed that she blamed herself
for what had happened. What troubled him was that her
confession might be a screen behind which lay concealed
something she dared not admit.

Nevertheless, it was still none of his business. Above all
else, she had confided in him and he had betrayed her
confidence.

Through his thoughts he could hear his own voice saying
'. . . *You have my promise. Whatever you tell me will be
strictly confidential . . . providing I'm not questioned by the
police . . .'*

The fact that he had been questioned was neither excuse
nor consolation. Now he had to go on. Whatever he did he
could cause no more harm than he had already done. And
there was just the chance he could salvage something out of
the wreck of Robert Heseltine's life . . .

She was slower to answer the phone this time. Piper wondered if it were because she had no wish to hear what she
already knew. Yet that thought collapsed when he reminded
himself that she could easily have destroyed the letter.

He told her about Pauline Gordon and the old woman
without mentioning Inspector Cattanoch's suspicions. One
piece of bad news was enough for the time being.

Lynn's reaction was hardly what he had expected. In a
lifeless voice, she said, 'The whole world seems to have
turned upside down. I feel as if I'm living in a nightmare.
There's only one reason why this woman should've taken
her own life.'

'I can think of several reasons,' Piper said.

'You're merely trying to give me false comfort.'

'No, I'm not. It'll take more than Pauline Gordon's suicide to convince me that Robert ran away because he'd been
involved with her.'

'Why else would she do it? Two things she says in her

letter explain the kind of mood she was in. Read it again and you'll know I'm right.'

Piper had no need to read it. He remembered only too well.

. . . I cannot deny the love I have for you. It means more to me than life itself . . . You know I cannot live without you . . .

He said, 'Miss Gordon is believed to have died some time during Saturday afternoon. Even if they were having an affaire she couldn't have known then what was going to happen that night.'

With no feeling at all, Lynn asked, 'What difference does that make? Don't you see she must've phoned him after she'd spoken to me and he told her it was all over between them?'

'That may be how it looks. But I'm not convinced. My opinion is that the letter was written after she rang you and found she couldn't speak to Robert.'

'Does it matter? She knew they were finished. That phone call on Saturday morning may have been just a last despairing attempt to persuade him to change his mind.'

It was possible. Piper could find no argument against it. But so many things were based on Heseltine's disappearance. If he had not driven to the cliffs south of Little Mallet and there abandoned his car . . . if . . . if . . . if . . .

Only one explanation remained. Inspector Cattanoch must be right. Heseltine had silenced his mistress and then staged a fake suicide by leaving his jacket and cap on the edge of the cliffs.

But it was a poor explanation. No one would have suspected that Pauline had not taken her own life. If Heseltine were responsible he had arranged the killing so that he would be free of suspicion. He had no need to disappear, no need to throw away everything he had created for himself.

Nothing linked Pauline's death and the events at Little Mallet – nothing that would stand up to the light of reason.

Heseltine might have had a motive for killing Pauline Gordon but none for his subsequent behaviour.

Above all, the whole affair was out of character. Yet his wife would be finally convinced if she knew what Cattanoch had suggested. It might only be a matter of time before she got to know.

Piper said, 'When you talk like that you put me in a very awkward situation.'

With a little more energy in her voice, Lynn asked, 'Why? What else do you expect me to say?'

'Well, forgive me for putting it this way, but I'd expect you to have more faith in your husband. I'd hate to think my wife would condemn me unheard. Shouldn't you wait until you hear his side of the story?'

The question seemed to bring out all her suppressed emotion. She almost choked over the words as she said, 'You've no right to say a thing like that. I looked on you as a friend and —'

'I'm also Robert's friend,' Piper said.

'That doesn't allow you to criticize my feelings towards him. I've never known you talk like this before.'

'There's never been a situation where I had to. Please understand that I want to help in any way I can but it won't do any good to make snap judgments. I realize how you must feel while you're waiting for —'

'You don't. You haven't the faintest idea. Ask Jane how she would feel if she were in my position . . . ask Jane. Right now I want you to leave me alone. Sorry, John, but I can't take any more.'

Her voice broke. As he began to protest, she hung up.

Quinn's extension was engaged. He rang back ten minutes later as Piper was getting ready to go home.

'. . . Tried your number an hour ago but got no reply. How did you make out with Mrs Heseltine? Anything productive?'

'Too productive,' Piper said. 'Wish I'd stayed out of this business.'

'Sounds interesting. Going to tell me about it?'

'Yes . . . but not for publication.'

Quinn said, 'All right. I don't mind if you take the bread from my mouth. Let's hear what you've been up to . . .'

He interjected only one or two questions. The rest of the time he listened in silence.

When Piper had told him the whole story, he said, 'Large oaks from little acorns grow . . . Well, well, well. Quite a lad is your pal Robert Quentin Heseltine, quite a lad. Do you think he did wrong by our Pauline and had to shut her mouth?'

'No. Do you?'

'I doubt it. But before I bring the mighty brain to bear on our escapade, I'll tell you what I learned at the Brompton Clinic . . .'

Snatches from some of the things Dr Egan had said fixed themselves in Piper's mind. As a professional colleague of long standing, Egan's views were of value. Others merely guessed or suspected. He was in a position to know.

'. . . *I can't see him deliberately taking his own life because he had some kind of problem. Heseltine's never been the depressive type . . . Nearly always there are warning signs . . . and I've never seen anything to make me suspect he was a man who could commit suicide . . .*'

And another thing on which Egan had been quite positive: '. . . *He wasn't the sort of man to persuade himself he had some imaginary ailment.*'

Then later: '. . . *Anybody can make a mistake . . . accidents happen . . . but he's never blotted his copybook.*'

After Quinn had finished, Piper asked, 'Do you think Dr Egan could've been covering up for a friend?'

Quinn said, 'No, I don't. In my job you learn to spot evasion and I'd say Egan genuinely doesn't believe Heseltine would commit suicide.'

'But it's obvious he was worried, isn't it?'

'Could've been annoyance at being delayed.'

'According to Egan it was more than that.'

'Yes, but he admits he could be wrong. It was only an impression that he might not have thought worth mentioning if it hadn't been for what happened on Saturday night.'

'His impression may be significant because of what happened,' Piper said.

'Depends how you look at it. Now that we know Heseltine left the Clinic no later than a quarter to seven and had more than three hours to do the journey, my bet is that he stopped somewhere on the way and made a phone call.'

'You're merely guessing.'

'It's all guesswork. I'll hedge my bet by backing an outside chance that he met somebody.'

'If he did, the person he met didn't accompany him the rest of the way. He was alone when he'd almost reached the end of his journey.'

'True,' Quinn said. 'And none of this explains what we all want to know. Since he wasn't the type of man to commit suicide, what could make him do it . . . if he did it?'

'Pauline Gordon might be the answer,' Piper said.

'Not if he killed her. Assuming she was his fancy woman, he had nothing to fear once she was dead. It would look like suicide and no one would have any reason to think it wasn't suicide . . .'

Quinn had a fit of coughing. When he got his breath back, he asked, 'Incidentally, was he the sort of fellow who'd commit premeditated murder ?'

'The last man in the world,' Piper said.

'Then we'll leave that out. Now what are we left with?'

'The same two possibilities we started with: either he jumped off the cliff or he set the stage to make it look like that.'

'Because he'd decided that the time had come to get out,' Quinn said.

'So it would appear.'

'Better make up your mind. He wasn't carted off into outer space by a flying saucer.'

Piper thought of the lurking guilt at the back of Lynn Heseltine's eyes. The answer – or part of the answer – might lie there. She believed her husband had been having an affaire but she blamed herself for his infidelity. For some reason that only she knew she also felt responsible for what had happened to him.

An ugly idea intruded itself. Her self-condemnation might well be a pose. Perhaps she was responsible for what had happened. Perhaps she had made it happen . . .

The phone asked peevishly, 'Did you hear me or have we been cut off?'

'I was thinking of a third possibility,' Piper said.

'Such as what?'

'It's all rather nebulous and I don't want to make too much out of it . . .'

'Until I know what it is I can't make anything out of it . . . as the actress said to the bishop. Why not let me in on your profound thought?'

'Nothing very profound. Just an idea that Robert Heseltine may have arranged to meet somebody at the spot where they found his car.'

'That's not original. I had the same idea myself. What else goes with it?'

'The person he met may have been his wife,' Piper said.

'May have been – ' Quinn was interrupted by another bout of coughing.

Then he asked in a husky voice, 'What kind of friends have you got? Do you realize you're as good as saying she knocked off her husband?'

'No, I wouldn't go as far as that.'

'How far would you go? If she did meet him there's only one reason why he hasn't been seen since. I don't have to tell you he's down at the bottom of the deep blue sea . . . do I?'

'There could be another explanation.'

'But you can't think of one and neither can I. Wonder when the police will get round to asking her where she was on Saturday night?'

'You mustn't breathe a word of this,' Piper said. 'What I've been saying – '

'Is strictly confidential. I know without being told. So not to worry. It'll be our cute little secret.'

'Don't be silly. Frankly, I can't imagine Lynn Heseltine harming anyone . . . least of all Robert.'

Quinn said, 'You're forgetting the old adage about a woman scorned. She might've found out that Robert had strayed from the path of rectitude and she didn't fancy acting as one corner of a triangle . . . eh?'

'It doesn't fit in with what I know of her.'

'Neither does Heseltine's behaviour fit in with what you thought you knew of him. However, them wot live longest learn most. I'll probably see you at the inquest on Miss Pauline Gordon. Have you inquired about her mother?'

'Yes. They think she'll recover.'

'If she does, she may shed some light on the events of Saturday afternoon. Who knows? Maybe the Gordon woman's phone call that morning set things really going. Maybe she got an unexpected visitor a little later on . . . and I don't mean lover-boy.'

Piper said, 'Now you are getting beyond yourself.'

'Think so?' Quinn broke off to clear his throat. 'Why couldn't it have been a woman who held the pillow over poor Pauline's face and slit open her wrist?'

'The woman we've been talking about wouldn't have the strength. Apart from which, how would she get herself invited upstairs to the bedroom?'

Quinn said, 'A very good question, Mr Piper, sir. I'll add it to my growing collection. And now I must regretfully bid you avoirdupois. My watch says they've been open these past fifteen minutes . . .'

CHAPTER IX

INQUIRIES into the disappearance of Robert Heseltine continued throughout Tuesday, August 23, but there were no new developments. When Quinn phoned Dorchester he learned that the position was unchanged.

Downey said the local police were disinclined to accept the theory that Heseltine had staged a fake suicide. Nothing in his social or professional background provided a motive.

'. . . They're convinced he'd have had to plan the whole thing very carefully and events indicate quite the reverse. He couldn't have known in advance he'd be called on to perform an emergency operation that afternoon so all his arrangements were made on the presumption that he'd be leaving London hours before he actually did leave and –'

'He'd have reached Dorchester long before nightfall,' Quinn said.

'Quite. Since it was a lovely day there were bound to be some people around and he'd have been seen . . . more than likely. To get to where the car was parked he had to leave the road, cross a footpath and ride on to a grass verge pretty near the edge of the cliff. Couldn't do that without being noticed.'

'Have you visited the spot?'

'Yes. If Heseltine planned to go there he must've known something about the area and I can't see him imagining he wouldn't attract attention.'

'What if he didn't care who saw him?'

'Perhaps he didn't. But why go all that way?'

'The point you're making is the same as mine,' Quinn said. 'It wasn't planned. Therefore he learned something on the journey that forced him to do what he wouldn't normally have dreamed of doing.'

'And he probably didn't arrive at a final decision until he was almost at Dorchester.'

'That's about the size of it.'

Quinn asked himself if all his ideas might not dovetail into one composite solution. Maybe Lynn Heseltine had got rid of Miss Gordon. A certain kind of woman might go to any lengths to save her husband from the results of his folly.

. . . *Suppose – for reasons that may be unimportant – Heseltine phoned his wife from a call box on the way to Dorchester? And suppose she told him what she'd done? The knowledge that it had all come about because he'd betrayed her might've driven him to sacrifice himself in the hope that everybody would believe he'd killed his mistress and then committed suicide because of remorse . . .*

As a concept it was bizarre – a travesty of what real people did in a real situation. Quinn felt it had no more substance than one of those TV crimes of passion that the public were gulled into accepting as everyday events in France.

And yet it could be . . . it just could be. It was more plausible than the notion that two people who had shared an illicit association had committed suicide on the same day. Coincidences did happen. But that would be straining credibility too far.

Downey said, 'You don't sound too sure. Why not come down here and take a look around for yourself?'

'It wouldn't achieve anything,' Quinn said. 'When you let me know they've found Robert Heseltine, that'll be the time. Just let's keep hoping they do find him . . .'

Detective-Inspector Cattanoch admitted he had read Quinn's Column on Crime. '. . . Very entertaining, I must say. Your approach is somewhat different from others of its kind.'

It could have been meant as a compliment but Quinn

had his doubts. He said, 'That might be called damning
with faint praise, but *chacun à son goût*. One cannot be all
things to all men . . . whatever that may mean. Right now
I'd be grateful for a mite of information on the death of a
Pauline Gordon who departed this life through a cut wrist.'

'There's nothing to tell you that hasn't already been re-
leased to the Press. There was a paragraph about it in your
own paper this morning.'

'Ah, but none of the papers mentioned a letter she wrote
to a certain medical gent who was last seen on Saturday
night,' Quinn said.

The phone hummed and crackled while Cattanoch decided what he should say. Then he asked, 'Who told you
she wrote any letter?'

'An insurance assessor I've known for a long time. He
confides in me now and again on the understanding that it
goes no further. Having read today's *Morning Post* you'll
agree that it hasn't.'

In an offhand voice, Cattanoch asked, 'If you know
about it, what do you want from me?'

'Just the answer to a simple question. Have you told the
Dorchester police what she wrote to the man who disappeared last Saturday night?'

This time the inspector had no trouble in finding an
answer. He said, 'I'm afraid that's a confidential matter
between two police departments.'

'So I'd imagine. Dorchester are keeping it so confidential
anybody'd think the letter didn't exist.'

Cattanoch said, 'I expect they know what they're doing.'

'Wish I did. When is the inquest being held on Pauline
Gordon? Or is that top secret as well?'

'No secret at all. Ten-thirty tomorrow morning. Chelsea
Coroner's Court. Will you be there?'

'That you can bet your shirt on,' Quinn said.

Only two other reporters were covering the inquest.
Quinn knew neither of them. He sat alone in the front row

of the press box and watched the public section as the minute hand of the clock above the door moved on to half past ten.

Few people seemed to be interested in the death of a woman called Pauline Gordon. They were the usual type : some elderly men with nothing better to occupy their time; a dozen women, mostly in couples. Half the benches were empty when the coroner took his seat.

Piper had arrived ten minutes before the proceedings began. Quinn saw him exchange a word with a red-headed police sergeant and a tall thin man with sparse hair and a sober face.

The jury were sworn . . . there was a whispered conversation between the coroner and one or two officials. Then Sergeant Hannan was called.

He stated that he had been on patrol duty in the neighbourhood of Northwood Avenue off the Fulham Road on Monday, August 22, at about three-fifteen in the afternoon. As he approached the telephone box at the top end of Northwood Avenue he was stopped by a man who requested assistance.

'. . . According to what he told me there was reason to believe that someone living at 56 Northwood Avenue had been taken ill. This person was understood to be alone in the house. The man informed me that he was John Piper, an insurance assessor, and he had called at number 56 to see a Miss Pauline Gordon who resided there.'

When Sergeant Hannan paused to turn over a page in his notebook, the coroner asked, 'Did Mr Piper say if he had called by appointment?'

'Not at that time, sir. But I learned later that Miss Gordon had not been expecting him.'

'Very good, Sergeant. Please continue.'

'Well, sir, I advised Mr Piper to drive back to the house and I would follow him in the police car. On arriving there I was unable to get any reply although I could hear the sounds of distress that Mr Piper told me he'd heard . . .'

The jury listened to Sergeant Hannan's account of the newspaper in the letter box and the untouched bottle of milk. He described how he had made forcible entry, gone upstairs to one of the bedrooms and found an old woman lying on the floor in her nightdress.

'Was she conscious?'

'Not really, sir. In a pretty bad way, from what I could see. I got the impression she'd fallen and injured herself. To me it looked as if she hadn't had anything to eat or drink for a long time.'

'What did you do then?'

'While Mr Piper was fetching a glass of water I made her as comfortable as I could without disturbing her too much. There wasn't anything to be done after that except get proper medical attention and I was waiting for the ambulance to arrive when Mr Piper called to me from the room next door . . .'

His description of the state in which he had found Pauline Gordon left very little to the imagination. When asked if he had noticed any sign of disturbance in the room he said everything appeared to be all right.

'Was the deceased in bed . . . that is, covered by the bedclothes?'

'No, sir. She was lying on the bed – fully dressed except for her shoes.'

'And you say she was holding a small knife?'

'In her right hand, sir.'

'Did you touch her at all?'

'Never went nearer than a couple of feet from the bed, sir. I knew there was nothing anyone could do for her. It was easy to see she'd been dead for quite some time.'

The coroner said, 'Thank you, Sergeant. I think that will be all at this stage . . .'

John Piper's evidence added little that the court had not already heard. His reason for visiting 56 Northwood Avenue was referred to only in passing.

'. . . I'd never met Miss Gordon personally. I got her name and address from a letter she'd written to some people I know.'

'You visited the house on the off-chance that she'd be at home?'

'More or less. I'd have rung to make an appointment but she wasn't in the phone book.'

'When you got no reply, what did you do, Mr Piper?'

'I spoke to the next-door neighbour at number 58. She told me she hadn't seen Miss Gordon that day. The sounds I could hear inside the house would probably be Mrs Gordon who suffered from arthritis and wasn't very mobile. That was why she hadn't answered the door.'

'What were these sounds you'd heard?'

'Like somebody in pain. I thought at first they were a child crying but, when I went back and listened again, I decided it was possible that Mrs Gordon had been taken ill and her daughter had gone for the doctor. The lady at number 58 told me the nearest phone box was at the top of the avenue. So I waited.'

'But, of course, Miss Gordon didn't return.'

'No. After I'd allowed what I considered was ample time, I felt the best thing to do was to get in touch with the police. I just couldn't ignore the possibility that an old person was badly in need of help . . .'

The rest confirmed Sergeant Hannan's statement. It was when Piper was describing his discovery of Pauline Gordon's body that the coroner asked, 'What made you go into the adjoining bedroom?'

'Curiosity, more than anything else. I'd begun to think Miss Gordon had packed up and left, perhaps because she'd had a quarrel with her mother. Quite obviously the old lady had been alone in the house since the previous day, at least. That was Sergeant Hannan's opinion, too. Everything did seem to indicate that they'd had a row and Miss Gordon had gone off.'

Quinn sensed a change in the atmosphere of the court. It

affected the coroner's dry voice, as he asked, 'Did you suspect that something much more serious might've occurred?'

'Not at all. What I saw when I opened the bedroom door
came as a very great shock. I'd expected only to find open
drawers and other signs that she'd taken her things and
gone.'

'Did you make any attempt to verify that she was dead?'

Under his breath, Quinn murmured, 'What he's really
asking is whether you disturbed the body. That dry old
stick knows more than he wants the jury to know.'

Piper said, 'It wasn't necessary. The extent of the wound
in her wrist and the fact that it had stopped bleeding told
me enough. I'd only taken a step or two into the room but I
saw all I needed to see.'

The coroner nodded, turned to look at the jury and
asked, 'Have you any questions for this witness?'

There were no questions. As he went back to his seat,
Piper caught sight of Quinn and gave him a half-smile –
the kind of smile that looked strained. Quinn could guess
Piper was relieved his public interrogation was over.

Mrs Marion Earley told the coroner she had lived at
number 58 Northwood Avenue for the past twelve years
and had known the Gordons for the major part of that
time. They were quiet-living people who had never had
much to do with their neighbours.

'. . . Pleasant enough but kept themselves to themselves –
if you know what I mean.'

'Have you ever heard them refer to other members of
their family?'

'No. From what I've been able to gather there aren't
any. Just the two of them. Mr Gordon died many years ago
before we took the house next door.'

'So mother and daughter have lived alone together all
the time you've known them?'

'Yes.'

'Any friends?'

'None that I know of.' Mrs Earley had a moment's

trouble with her dentures. 'Never seen people visiting them
. . . although, of course, somebody might've done.'

'But no regular visitors?'

'No. If there had been I'm bound to have noticed it . . .
seeing we've been next-door neighbours for such a long
time.'

The coroner made a brief note on his desk pad. Then he
said, 'The reason for these questions, Mrs Earley, is that
you would appear to be the only available person who has
known both mother and daughter for many years. In the
circumstances, this court is entitled to accept your identification of the deceased.'

Mrs Earley's plump face took on a look of importance.
She said, 'Well, one thing I can say is that I saw her often
enough.'

'Precisely.' He consulted his notes. 'Were you asked by
the police to visit the local mortuary yesterday, August 23?'

'Yes, they called for me in a police car.'

'And were you there shown the body of a woman?'

In a more subdued voice, Mrs Earley said, 'Yes.'

'Who was the woman?'

'Miss Gordon – Pauline Gordon.'

'You are quite sure of that?'

'Absolutely positive. After knowing her all these years
I'm not likely to make a mistake.'

'Thank you, Mrs Earley. That will be all.'

The next witness was a Dr Franklin Kissane. He had a
round red face and he was almost completely bald.

When asked to state his professional qualification he said
he was a qualified medical practitioner. For the past six
years, he had served as police surgeon for the district.

'On Monday, August 22, were you called to a dwelling
house situate at 56 Northwood Avenue, SW10?'

'Yes, sir, I was.'

'Tell us, Doctor, what happened when you got there.'

'In an upstairs bedroom I found the body of a woman

believed to be Miss Pauline Gordon. On examination I formed the opinion that death had taken place between thirty-six and forty-eight hours previously. Various factors inclined me to the view that the latter figure would be the more accurate.'

'Was this view confirmed by a subsequent post-mortem examination?'

'It was, sir. The findings of Professor Mortimer White of the Home Office tallied with my original estimate.'

The coroner nodded like a man who had known the answer without asking. He said, 'Since Professor White is shortly to give evidence before this court, you may confine yourself, Doctor, to the conclusions you came to on Monday afternoon. What opinion did you form as to the cause of death?'

Dr Kissane referred to a small pocket diary before he said, 'The deceased had a deep wound in the left wrist. It had been made by two – or possibly three – incisions by a sharp instrument and was of such a nature as to sever both the ulnar and the radial arteries.'

'What would the immediate results be of this type of wound?'

'Well, rapid loss of blood would soon result in unconsciousness. I should say that death must have occurred within a very few minutes.'

Once again the coroner made some notes in a slow careful hand. Then he asked with deliberate emphasis, 'Did you notice any other injuries on the body?'

'Nothing obvious.'

'No bruising of the arms or face which might indicate that there had been a struggle?'

'Not that I could see. Except for her shoes she was completely dressed and her clothing was in no way disturbed.'

'We have been told that she had a knife in her right hand. Could it have caused the incisions to which you have referred?'

'Yes, sir. It was sharp enough. I found bloodstains on the cutting edge.'

'Was the knife firmly gripped in her hand?'

'No, rather loosely.'

'Did that indicate anything to you?'

'Only that her grasp probably relaxed when she became unconscious.'

The coroner nodded and leaned back. He asked, 'Is there anything else you think the jury should know?'

'Well, I found what appeared to be saliva on the pillow under her head. Laboratory tests revealed that it was, indeed, saliva and it had come from the dead woman's mouth.'

'What conclusions do you draw from that?'

'Only one. Since her head was turned sideways on the pillow, it is likely that a certain amount of saliva would trickle out of her mouth as she was losing consciousness. It happens often when a person is completely relaxed in sleep.'

With no change of tone, the coroner asked, 'Could it have happened in this case if her nose and mouth had been covered with the pillow?'

Dr Kissane smoothed a hand over his shiny bald head. While he took time to consider his answer, the six men and three women on the jury watched him intently.

At last, he said, 'Yes, I would say it could. But I saw nothing to substantiate any idea that violence had been used against the deceased, other than the injury caused by the knife in her hand.'

'So it is your considered opinion, Doctor, that the wound in her wrist was self-inflicted?'

'It is.'

The jury had no questions. Because of professional demands on his time, Dr Kissane was excused further attendance.

Professor Mortimer White had sharp blue eyes and a pink-and-white complexion. His manner was that of a man accustomed to authority.

He stated that he had carried out a post-mortem examination on the body of a woman named on the coroner's order as Pauline Gordon. She had then been dead between two and three days.

'. . . My examination was made at eight p.m. on Monday, August 22. Various indications – taken in conjunction with the warm weather of the past week – led me to the conclusion that death had probably occurred some time before Saturday evening.'

'Did you find any symptoms of disease?'

'No. She was between forty and forty-five years of age, reasonably well-nourished and of normal physique. I am of the opinion, however, that she suffered from a depressive ailment. In the stomach contents I found traces of amitriptyline hydrochloride which is a tricyclic anti-depressant commonly prescribed for anxiety states.'

The coroner glanced at the jury with no change of expression on his lined, narrow face. Then he asked, 'Are persons for whom such a drug is prescribed of the type to commit suicide?'

'There are varying stages of depression,' Professor White said.

'But would you say a depressive illness carries that risk?'

'Well, I'd say that suicidal tendencies have always to be watched for.'

The coroner's tight smile was lacking in humour. He said, 'I'd suggest that is a distinction with very little difference. However, let us turn to something more practical. What conclusions did you reach as to the cause of death?'

Professor White rested both hands on the rail of the witness box and hunched up his shoulders. He said, 'She died from a massive external haemorrhage. A wound in her left wrist had severed both arteries and she was almost completely exsanguinated.'

'Could this wound have been self-inflicted?'

'Oh yes. From its nature and a lack of any contra-indications, I would have no hesitation in saying that it was.'

'You examined the knife that we have been told was found loosely held in her other hand?'

'Yes. It was the kind of weapon I'd have expected. As a matter of routine I checked the bloodstains on the blade. They belonged to the same blood group as that of the deceased.'

'Very well, Professor. Is there anything else you wish to add?'

'Only what you will find stated in my post-mortem examination report. The autopsy findings are consistent with deliberate self-inflicted wounding and give no cause for suspicion.'

The coroner said, 'Thank you, Professor. I am sure your evidence will assist the jury in arriving at a proper verdict.'

Detective-Inspector Cattanoch was the last witness. He described what he had seen on arrival at 56 Northwood Avenue and the condition of the bedroom in which Pauline Gordon had been found dead.

'. . . No signs of any disturbance and nothing to suggest that she had been assaulted. She was fully dressed but for her shoes. These were under the edge of the bed where they had been neatly placed side by side.'

'There was a small knife in her right hand?'

'Yes, sir.'

'Anything unusual about it in your experience?'

'No, sir. Most domestic kitchens have one or more of them. They're generally called vegetable knives.'

'Have you been able to ascertain if such a knife was used in the home of the deceased?'

'I'm afraid not, sir. The only person who might be expected to know is Mrs Gordon, mother of the deceased, and she is still not in a fit state to be questioned.'

'What other inquiries have you made, Inspector?'

'I've spoken, sir, to Pauline Gordon's doctor. He confirms that he's been prescribing anti-depressant drugs for the deceased over quite a long period. If you would like him to give evidence –'

'No, I don't think that will be necessary.' The coroner looked at the jury questioningly and nine pairs of eyes looked back at him in agreement. 'I have only one more question. Was there anything about the circumstances of Miss Gordon's death or the state of her bedroom to make you suspect that this might not be a case of suicide?'

Inspector Cattanoch needed a few seconds to consider his answer. Then he said, 'No, sir.'

The coroner's remarks were brief but comprehensive. After a whispered conference among themselves the jury returned a verdict that the deceased had died from incisions in the wrist, self-inflicted while the balance of her mind was disturbed.

CHAPTER X

As QUINN LEFT the courtroom, Piper was just ahead of him. They halted outside on the steps leading down to the pavement.

It was another warm, sunlit day but there had been a forecast of rain before evening. Over to the west a bank of cloud had already formed in an otherwise empty sky.

Quinn said, 'To coin a phrase, the law has not only to be done but has to be seen to be done.'

'You mean justice, not law,' Piper said.

'Maybe I do. Then again maybe I don't. Perhaps justice didn't enter into the proceedings. Perhaps we've just witnessed the law being done and done proper.'

'You don't agree with the verdict?'

'It's not for me to question the findings of nine good citizens and true. All the same I wonder what they'd have thought of the letter that poor Pauline wrote shortly before her death.'

'They might well have considered that it showed beyond any doubt her state of mind.'

'Nevertheless, the fact that she died and Heseltine disappeared on the same day might've struck them as a bit of a coincidence.'

'Life's full of coincidences,' Piper said.

'Sententious if not original.' Quinn caught sight of Detective-Inspector Cattanoch in the doorway. 'Here comes a pal of yours . . . the copper wot wasn't sure how he should answer the coroner's final question.'

Cattanoch paused on his way down the steps. He said, 'I thought you'd have been gone by now, Mr Piper. What's your opinion of the verdict?'

'Same as yours, I imagine. Why didn't you ask for an adjournment?'

'Wouldn't have served any purpose. Plenty of time to re-open the affair if a certain missing gentleman turns up.'

With something near to a smile on his long thin face he glanced sideways at Quinn and asked, 'What does the *Morning Post*'s crime correspondent think?'

Quinn said, 'I'm flattered. How did you find out who I was?'

'Someone told me – someone who was curious to know why a man who deals mostly in big time should concern himself with small time. In any case, I expected you to attend the inquest after what you said on the phone.'

'Yes, of course. Mind telling me something strictly off the record?'

'Depends on the something and if you're entitled to know.'

'It's this: what else did Pauline's doctor say about her, apart from the fact that she'd been receiving treatment for depression?'

Cattanoch said, 'Nothing very much. He'd had the opinion she was stuck on some man but he put it down to her emotional condition. Her age and her circumstances would be inclined to give her fanciful ideas.'

'Such as a crush on the surgeon who'd operated on her?'

'Well, yes. It was an operation for some female complaint and she told the GP that Mr Heseltine was the only one who'd ever done anything for her. Was always talking about him.'

'Does the GP think her feelings were reciprocated?'

'No. He says it's a common thing with frustrated spinsters. Many a doctor gets pestered by that kind of woman patient . . . especially psychiatrists. The gynaecologist comes across it quite often, too.'

'So Pauline was merely feeding on a delusion,' Quinn said.

Inspector Cattanoch shrugged. He said, 'That's how it seems to add up. However, if the whole thing was a baseless infatuation, perhaps you'd tell me something now.'

He glanced from Quinn to Piper and back to Quinn again. Then he asked, 'What made Robert Heseltine do what he did last Saturday night if he wasn't afraid that Miss Gordon could make trouble for him?'

Far back in Piper's mind he could hear a snatch of his conversation with Lynn Heseltine. Standing out above all else had been her discomfort when asked a simple question.

'. . . *How did you come to drift apart?*'

And her answer had been a patent evasion. '. . . *I can't even remember how it all began. Grew out of nothing, really . . .*'

Then Quinn said, 'We don't know what Heseltine did after he parked his car near the edge of the cliff. He may have jumped into the sea or gone for a walk in the moonlight or ascended in a chariot of fire like the prophet Elijah. So not knowing what we can't even guess why.'

'You're not very helpful,' Cattanoch said.

'I'm doing the best I can with rather limited material . . . as the curate said on his wedding night. Until Heseltine turns up we can only sit twiddling our thumbs. Are you a twiddler?'

Piper said, 'Pay no attention to him, Inspector. My opinion is that the jury brought in a true verdict.'

'Does that mean –' Cattanoch scratched the ridge of his lean jaw – 'that you don't believe there was any connection between Pauline Gordon's death and Heseltine's disappearance?'

'Ah, now you're going just a bit too far.'

'Well, you can't have it both ways. Either there was or there wasn't.'

'He likes to sit on the fence,' Quinn said. 'Always reminds me of a well-known politician who's done it so often he has a ridge in his posterior.'

The inspector's mouth twitched in another elusive smile. He said, 'Maybe Mr Piper will come down off the fence when I tell him I've spoken to Robert Heseltine's secretary at the Brompton Clinic. She remembers a phone call he received last Saturday morning.'

Piper had a feeling of inevitability. He asked, 'From Miss Gordon?'

'Yes. She said it was a private matter and she wanted to speak to him personally. What stuck in the secretary's mind is that he seemed extremely annoyed.'

'Did she overhear the conversation?'

'Only an odd word or two which didn't convey anything. But when he hung up she heard him say ". . . Damn the woman." That's mainly why she remembered the incident.'

'Also explains why Pauline wrote that letter,' Quinn said. 'Now the question is whether she meant to make a first-class nuisance of herself . . .'

'Or?'

'Or if it were the sort of thing they call a despairing cry for help.'

'I prefer that explanation,' Piper said.

Inspector Cattanoch scratched his jaw again. He said, 'Unless Heseltine comes back from wherever he's gone, I'm inclined to think we'll never know. Won't be the first time, either. Good day, gentlemen . . .'

He gave them an abrupt nod, trotted down the steps and got into a police car. The sudden change in his manner was very noticeable.

Quinn said, 'Coppers don't go much for blind loyalty. The inspector evidently disapproves of the faith you show in your friend Heseltine.'

'A man's innocent until he's proved guilty,' Piper said. 'I wonder if Heseltine mentioned anything about Pauline Gordon when he talked with Dr Egan at . . . what time was it?'

'About six o'clock. They met outside the operating theatre where Heseltine had been doing an appendicectomy.'

'That was when he gave the impression he was worried about something?'

'Yes. But Egan told me he had no idea why Heseltine was worried.'

'Perhaps it didn't strike Egan as the kind of thing to worry about.'

'Or to talk about,' Quinn said.

A picture of the look on Lynn's face came between Piper and his next thought. Then it was gone.

He said, 'I haven't told you this before but I'm almost sure Mrs Heseltine wasn't being completely frank with me. That letter wasn't the only thing she'd wanted to keep secret.'

'It was bad enough. What else could there be?'

'I don't know. And it would be useless to ask her. The only hope is that Egan may have some clue without realizing it.'

'Want me to have another word with him?'

'No, I'll do it myself,' Piper said.

As soon as he got back to his office he rang Egan's consulting rooms. A woman's voice answered. She sounded young, cool and self-possessed.

'. . . He's attending to a patient right now. Can I help you?'

'No, thank you. This isn't a professional matter. Dr Egan knows who I am. When d'you think he'll be available?'

'Not for another fifteen or twenty minutes . . . at a guess. Then he's due at the Brompton Clinic. If you'd care to give me a message . . .'

'Please ask him to phone me before he leaves,' Piper said. 'He's got my number. You can say it's rather important.'

It was close on half past one when Egan phoned. He said, 'Nice to hear from you. Had a visit from a friend of yours the other day. Somebody by the name of Quinn. Does crime stuff for the *Morning Post*.'

'Yes, I know. He wanted background material on Robert Heseltine and I suggested he might talk to Stone, the ENT man. Apparently Stone wouldn't agree to be interviewed and so you had to give up your time instead.'

'Oh, I didn't mind. Stone is inclined to be boorish. Nearly as bad as the orthopaedics.'

After a slight hesitation, Egan added, 'Bad business this Heseltine affair. Have you spoken to his wife?'

'Yes, a couple of days ago. Haven't been in touch with her since.'

'How's she taking it?'

'Pretty hard. Could you and I have a private chat about it some time today?'

'If you think it would do any good . . . Let me see what appointments I've got.'

His voice receded from the phone and all Piper could hear was the rustling of papers at the other end. Then Egan said, 'I'm going to the Brompton Clinic very shortly and I won't be coming back here. But I can see you there about three-thirty. That all right?'

'Suit me fine,' Piper said.

He spent half an hour on some paper work before he went to lunch. Just after half past three a taxi dropped him at the main entrance of the Clinic.

Someone directed him to the Radio-Therapy department. Someone else told him Dr Egan had gone to X-ray but would be back soon.

Piper waited in the long passage where complicated pieces of equipment were parked outside various doors. He passed the time studying dials and meters that he could never hope to understand.

At a quarter to four Egan arrived. He apologized for the delay, gave Piper a warm handshake and said, 'Hope you won't mind but I can only spare five or ten minutes. It's one of those days.'

'This shouldn't take long,' Piper said.

'Good. Let's find a room where there's a phone. When we've had our talk I want to ring my receptionist.'

He was not quite as tall as Piper but broader in the shoulder and fair-skinned to match his auburn hair. In voice

and manner he had the quiet confidence of a man who had
no need to assert himself.

On their way along the corridor he made some remark
about the weather and seemed to be deliberately avoiding
any reference to Robert Heseltine. Piper wondered how
Egan felt at the disappearance of a colleague with whom
he had worked for some years.

*. . . Perhaps medical men can discipline their feelings.
Often heard them say the one thing they must never do is
to become emotionally involved. Always thought that ap-
plied to patients but maybe it works with personal rela-
tionships as well. Suppose you have to learn to control yourself . . .*

As they turned the corner they almost bumped into a
fair-haired pretty girl with a shy smile that made her look
very young. Egan asked, 'Where are you going in such a
hurry?'

'I'm looking for Mr Stone. You haven't seen him by any
chance?'

'Not since I got here. And that's at least an hour ago. So
I'm afraid I can't help you.'

Egan saw her give Piper a second look. He said, 'Oh, let
me introduce you. This is John Piper, a friend of mine.
Christine Bowater . . . one of Stone's surgical team.'

She offered Piper her hand and smiled shyly. She asked,
'Are you a policeman?'

'No . . . but you're not the first person to mistake me for
one. As it happens I'm in the insurance business.'

'Oh, you're the – ' she looked at him wide-eyed – 'the
assessor whose name I've seen in the papers quite a few
times . . . aren't you?'

Piper said, 'Yes. It's the penalty of becoming involved
in notorious affairs that receive a lot of publicity.'

'We've had – ' her youthful smile faded – 'more than
our share of that recently. You know what's happened, I
suppose?'

'Yes. All very distressing. I've been on friendly terms

with Robert Heseltine for some years. Did you see him at all last Saturday?'

'Only in passing. I had a day off and didn't have to come on duty until seven o'clock. Got here about a quarter to seven and saw Mr Heseltine driving away as I parked my car.'

'Was he alone?'

'Oh yes. I'm sure of that. There was no one else with him.'

'Anything unusual about him that you remember? I mean, did he look ill or upset?'

'Not that I noticed. Of course, I was a short distance away from him and he was wearing his sun-glasses . . . but he seemed all right to me.'

With a hint of sadness in her eyes, she added, 'I hope nothing really bad has happened to him. However, I must go now. Nice to have met you, Mr Piper . . .'

When she had gone out of sight, Egan said, 'That's the most puzzling feature of this whole business. Everybody likes Heseltine. I've never met anyone who could wish him harm. Always friendly and sociable.'

'Certainly no pomposity about him,' Piper said.

'Not like – ' Egan lowered his voice – 'like an ENT man I could mention. Different type altogether. Makes you wonder.'

He led the way to a door marked: *PRIVATE*. As he ushered Piper in ahead of him, he said, 'We won't be disturbed in here. It's not often used.'

The room was furnished like most rooms of its kind in a hospital: it had three straight-backed chairs, a metal filing cabinet, an examination couch and a flat-topped desk with a telephone and some bulky manilla files.

Egan asked, 'Want to sit down?'

'No, thanks. I won't keep you long. My main reason for getting in touch with you was to talk about a woman called Pauline Gordon. Did Heseltine ever mention her?'

The blank look that came into Egan's face told Piper

the answer he was seeking would not be found here. It seemed obvious that Heseltine had confided neither in his wife nor one of his close colleagues.

'Not to me,' Egan said. 'I've never heard of her. Who is she?'

'One of Heseltine's patients. He operated on her some time ago. Don't know exactly when. What I do know is she behaved as though there was more than a professional relationship between them.'

'Oh, she did, did she? Well, I don't need to tell you she's talking poppycock. That sort of allegation is one of the hazards of our trade. Every medical man learns to guard against it and –'

There Egan stopped abruptly. In a changed tone, he asked, 'Are you suggesting Heseltine's disappearance is in some way connected with this woman Gordon?'

'It's not my suggestion,' Piper said. 'Personally, I just can't believe it. But things have happened in the past few days that are beginning to make people think it's possible.'

'Which people?'

'Well, on Monday his wife received a letter addressed to him. It was from this Pauline Gordon and it more or less spelled out that they'd been having an affair. The police have seen the letter and they think it ties in with the events of Saturday night when Heseltine abandoned his car on the cliffs near Little Mallet.'

Egan stood thinking for a long time, his smooth good-looking face set in a frown. Then he asked, 'Why did his wife show them the letter?'

'She didn't. I did. Circumstances arose that gave me no choice.'

'What circumstances?'

'After I'd seen it I got her permission to call on Miss Gordon. When I got to the house . . .'

With his arms folded and his mouth drawn in, Egan listened. Every now and again he moved restlessly.

'. . . The inquest took place this morning and they

brought in a verdict of suicide. In view of all the evidence they could hardly have returned any other verdict.'

'Were they told about the letter she'd written to Heseltine?'

'No. The police seem to feel it wouldn't have served any useful purpose.'

'Why not?'

'Because it would merely have provided the jury with even more justification for a verdict of suicide.'

'And dragged Robert Heseltine's name in the gutter,' Egan said. 'You're lucky things turned out as they did.'

Piper resented the implication. There might be a measure of reason for it but not enough to put all the blame on him.

He said, 'I wasn't responsible for the course of events. I thought I was acting in Robert's interests.'

'No doubt. I wouldn't question that. But you've heard the saying that the road to hell is oft paved with good intentions, haven't you?'

The easy tone of friendship in Egan's voice had gone. He sounded close to anger.

'It's easy to be wise with hindsight,' Piper said.

'That's a matter of opinion. I'd say you'd have done better not to go anywhere near this woman Gordon. Whatever way you look at it you weren't doing Robert a favour.'

'I wasn't to know what I'd find at the house in Northwood Avenue.'

'All right. Have it your own way.'

Egan's hostility lasted only a moment longer. Then he smoothed a hand over his thick auburn hair and looked sheepish.

He said, 'Sorry. I shouldn't have opened a big mouth. I know you and Robert Heseltine have been pretty friendly and you considered what you were doing was for the best. Besides, I don't suppose it can do any harm if the letter doesn't become public knowlelge. That's the important thing.'

'Not quite,' Piper said. 'Whatever may, or may not, have happened to Robert, I like to think that my decision to call on Pauline Gordon was the means of saving an old woman's life.'

'You're right. That's one real dividend.'

With some warmth in his voice, Egan added, 'I should've thought of it myself. To be frank, this affair's been niggling at me more than you'd believe. Between ourselves, that fellow Stone hasn't been making things any easier.'

'Why? What's he done?'

'Well, you know yourself how damn pompous he can be . . . and he's never really got on with Heseltine. Now he says the man's brought disrepute on the profession and damaged the Clinic by his unsavoury conduct and . . . oh, a lot of stuff like that. Anybody'd think Robert had done it deliberately.'

'Maybe he did,' Piper said. 'His wife thinks so. And she's not the only one. There's even a suggestion that either he staged his own disappearance or he jumped into the sea because he was responsible for the death of Pauline Gordon.'

A look of bewilderment narrowed Egan's eyes. He had to get rid of something in his throat before he said, 'Am I crazy or are you saying he killed her?'

'No, it isn't my idea. The very notion is absurd. But people do suspect that he may have been driven to shut her mouth because she was threatening to ruin him. From the tone of her letter he wanted to end their association and she wasn't prepared to let him go.'

Egan said, 'I don't get this at all. Didn't the inquest find that she'd taken her own life?'

'Yes. But it's still considered possible that the pillow could've been held over her face . . .'

The look of disbelief on Egan's face showed all too clearly what he was thinking while he listened. It tinged his voice when he said, 'I've only two comments to make. Holding a woman down while you cut her wrist would be damn difficult to do without leaving some marks of violent restraint. Secondly, nothing would ever get me to believe that Robert Heseltine could, or would, commit premeditated murder.'

'And that's what it would've had to be,' Piper said. 'If she didn't commit suicide, the knife must've been brought for the purpose of killing her.'

'And, from what both of us know of Robert Heseltine, it's absurd to imagine that anything could ever make him do such a thing.' Egan shrugged irritably. 'The whole idea's absolute nonsense. It's only put forward as a wild explanation for what happened on Saturday night.'

'Unfortunately there's no other explanation,' Piper said.

'There must be. It's bound to come out eventually. And we'll find that the answer's a simple one.'

'Usually it is. In this case, only Heseltine himself can provide the reason for what he did.'

Egan said, 'He might've stopped to make a phone call on his way to Dorchester. Your friend Quinn suggested that as a possibility. The trouble is it still doesn't explain why he drove to that spot and left his hat and jacket on the edge of the cliff.'

'Unless Quinn is right and Heseltine was given some news that left him no alternative.'

'I don't believe he'd take his own life.' Egan shook his head. 'I've known him too long for that. He wasn't the type of man to resort to suicide.'

'Well, it could hardly be accident,' Piper said. 'Something took place after he got out of his car. What do you think of the theory that he went there to meet somebody?'

Egan spent a moment in thought. Then he shook his head again.

He said, 'Can't see that. If there were anything in it at all it would mean they had a fight and Heseltine was pushed off the cliff. In that case, the police would've found signs of a struggle. And they didn't, did they?'

'Not to my knowledge. His jacket was nicely folded with

his cap on top of it. The driver's door of the Mercedes was open, the key was in the ignition. Apparently nothing had been taken from the car and nothing disturbed in it or around where it stood. If he didn't jump into the sea he's just vanished.'

'A man doesn't vanish like a ghost. Heseltine left here, drove to Dorchester and carried on until he came to the cliffs south of Winterbourne Abbas. It would seem he only stopped where he did because he could go no further.'

'Or because that's where he'd intended to go all along,' Piper said.

'Not when – ' there was no vestige of doubt in Egan's voice – 'when I spoke to him shortly before he left the Clinic. That time we met outside No. 3 theatre his sole intention was to visit his aunt in Dorchester. The only other thing I remember is that he was a bit annoyed at leaving later than he'd previously arranged.'

'So what changed his mind must've been something which happened on the journey,' Piper said.

'Yes, I suppose so.' Egan studied his watch. 'Looks like that, anyway. But talk wont get us very far . . . and you'll have to excuse me. I've got a lot to do and little enough time in which to do it.'

As he opened the door, he added, 'Let's hope something turns up pretty soon if only for his wife's sake.'

The thought that had troubled Piper once before returned to plague him again. He said, 'If you want my opinion she's lost all hope.'

Egan was going out but he stopped and looked back. He asked, 'What makes you say that?'

'She blames herself for the whole thing : Pauline Gordon's death and what happened to Robert.'

'Why should she be to blame?'

'Their relationship had gone wrong. Lynn Heseltine thinks it was at least partly her fault.'

'And the other part?'

'There seems no doubt in her mind that he was having

an affair with the Gordon woman.'

A disturbed look came into Egan's eyes. He said, 'She's a bit quick to condemn her husband. Not much faith in his integrity, has she?'

'That's what I told her. Of course, she's largely influenced by the letter which arrived Monday morning.'

'The wife of a medical man ought to know better.'

'Rather difficult to keep a balanced outlook in the circumstances,' Piper said.

Egan played with the knob of the door while he thought. Behind him someone went past along the corridor wheeling a trolley.

Then he asked, 'Can I tell you confidentially what I think?'

'Of course.'

'Well, there's quite a big disparity in age between Robert and his wife,' Egan said. 'I may be wrong but I don't believe she'll spend the rest of her life weeping if he doesn't come back . . .'

CHAPTER XI

THURSDAY, AUGUST 25, Quinn enjoyed a late morning in bed after a fairly thick night. By the time he got downstairs, Mrs Buchanan had gone out shopping.

He told himself that was one good thing. Her endless motherly advice would only aggravate his hangover.

'. . . Whit ye want is tae find yersel' some nice wee lassie who'll mak' ye a guid wife. That wid stop ye hanging aroon the pubs a' night. And Ah'm no haeing ye tell me ye canna afford to get wed. Ye could keep two wives on whit ye spend on the drink . . .'

A cup of hot strong coffee settled the aching in his head but the thought of eating repelled him. He could have his usual tea and toast when he got to the office. It was all his stomach would tolerate in the way of solid food.

That thought reminded him of the long-standing invitation Piper kept mentioning. Jane always wanted to know why he never got in touch with her.

'. . . *When are you going to come and have a meal with us? Any time you've got a free evening you'll be more than welcome. Just give me a ring the day before so that I'll expect you . . .*'

She had phoned him a couple of times but that was long ago. Perhaps she really had wanted him to visit them. Perhaps he should not have persuaded himself it was a duty invitation. He could scarcely blame her if she had given up trying. Now it was Piper who made the right noises whenever they met.

But not this time – not since Piper first rang him to ask about Heseltine. Probably Jane was out of town. Quite often she went to stay with friends for a few days. Jane was the sort of person who had a lot of friends . . . and Piper never seemed to mind being left on his own for a week or so.

Quinn idly wondered if Piper's marriage had really made much difference to their relationship. They had gone their separate ways even before then, meeting only at intervals when something of mutual interest cropped up. Socially they lived in different worlds.

Yet they understood each other and a strange loyalty existed between them. Nothing had ever altered that – not even when Piper re-married.

It was the only association that Quinn valued. He could remember no other that had lasted down through the years.

He was thinking of days gone by as he struggled into his raincoat and paused to look at himself in the hallstand mirror. What he saw depressed him.

People were right: he never changed. His reflection showed him the same limp, straw-coloured hair, thin pale face and tired eyes that looked back at him every morning while he was shaving.

. . . *You're as strong as a horse and yet anybody'd be entitled to think you had galloping TB. The clothes you wear don't help, either. Not much chance of you being nominated Best Dressed Man of the Year. If you keep that tie any longer it'll have antique value . . .*

There was little prospect of Mrs Buchanan seeing her hopes realized. No nice girl would look at him twice. And unless one did he would have no incentive to change his ways.

So it was the old question of the chicken and the egg and which came first. The right woman could make all the difference . . . if he found the right woman.

His reflection told him not to be stupid. A wife was not necessarily the answer. Take Robert Heseltine, for example . . .

There Quinn's thoughts shifted from himself to the man who had been missing for nearly five days. He was no advertisement for matrimony.

When he married he must have expected to live happily ever after. He had a successful career, a beautiful wife and ample money. A man could ask for no more.

And yet now he had nothing. He was nothing – just a name in the papers, a newspaper story that would be buried under a pile of other stories until it was forgotten.

Soon he would be forgotten, too, except by a handful of people whose lives had crossed his while he had been Robert Q. Heseltine, MSc., FRCS. Pity if it had all been thrown away for the sake of a woman . . . if his wife could be believed . . . if his wife could be believed . . .

She blamed herself for what had happened. Or so she had told Piper. It might not be the truth. It might only serve to conceal the truth. But either way it bore out that line by Thomas Kyd : *For what's a play without a woman in it?*

Perhaps there had been two women in Heseltine's life. Perhaps, on the other hand . . .

An idea soared up from the depths of Quinn's mind like a rocket heading for the stars. Before he had time to fix its position, to plot its course, it went out and left him in even greater darkness.

All that remained was the echo of a question : '. . . *Are you saying that Heseltine might've got a piece of disturbing news on the phone?*'

It could be the right question if it were put another way. He must have learned something profoundly disturbing either before or after he set off for Dorchester.

And it could hardly have been before. He had been annoyed, even irritable, but not in such a state as to do anything desperate.

Two women in his life . . . That was one too many. They called it the eternal triangle. Perhaps, in a sense, his wife had been telling the truth.

Quinn's reflection asked him what he hoped to make out of a fragment of an idea. It would be as much use as the tail of a rocket that had failed at take-off.

But he knew now that two people must have known the secret of Robert Heseltine's disappearance. And a woman called Pauline Gordon was not one of them. She had died before he left the hospital. In her own pathetic way she had been an incidental.

If no trace were ever found of Heseltine the mystery of his trip to the cliffs south of Little Mallet would remain a mystery. Some day he might return . . . some day. By then it would be too late for the truth ever to be revealed.

With a feeling that all things were for the worst, Quinn scowled at the mirror and went out. He was more than ever glad he had been deprived of Mrs Buchanan's company.

It had rained during the night but the streets were drying in the mid-morning sunshine. If he had not had a sour taste in his mouth and a lingering headache he would have been inclined to admit it was good to be alive.

At ten minutes to twelve he arrived at the office. Two cups of tea improved his spirits considerably. By the time he went down to the reporters' room he was fit to parry the usual comments on his appearance.

There was a note on his typewriter: IF YOU HAVE ANYTHING TO TELL ME I CAN GRANT YOU AN AUDIENCE AT ONE P.M. IF NOT, WHAT HAVE YOU BEEN DOING SINCE LAST WEEKEND?

He screwed the paper into a ball and sat tossing it from one hand to the other. Then he asked switchboard for a line and dialled Piper's number.

It was engaged. He got through when he tried a second time.

Piper said, 'I rang you an hour ago but they said you weren't in and I gathered you hadn't arrived yet. This your late turn?'

'Yes. Actually I'm not supposed to be here until some time between one and two but I had a couple of phone calls to make. You're the first. How did you get on with Thos. A. J. Egan?'

'Well, among other things, he doesn't place any faith in Pauline Gordon's letter. Gave me a mild telling-off for showing it to the police . . .'

Quinn drew interlocking doodles on a scrap of paper as he listened. He made no comment until he heard about the meeting with Christine Bowater and what she had seen when she came on duty Saturday evening.

Then he said, 'Pity she didn't speak to Heseltine before he drove off. We might have some idea what kind of mood he was in.'

'According to her he seemed all right. And I think he was.'

'Which means something happened on his way to Dorchester. When he set off he had no intention of driving to that spot on the cliffs.'

'So he must've stopped before he got to Dorchester.'

'And met someone.'

'More likely made a phone call. What he was told changed all his plans and he – '

'I'm not buying that,' Quinn said. 'I've thought all round this affair and I can't imagine what sort of news he could've been given that would make him drive miles past his destination for the sole purpose of jumping into the sea.'

Piper said, 'The only alternative is what I've already suggested. He met somebody on the cliffs near Little Mallet.'

'By prior arrangement? I can't see him doing that, either.'

'Perhaps he made the appointment by phone when he stopped on the way.'

'Why should they meet where his car was found?'

'It might've been the most suitable place if the person he phoned lived in Dorchester.'

'I wouldn't put my money on that one. He'd arranged a consultation with his aunt's GP. That's the only person he'd be likely to phone. And you can't convince me they'd choose Little Mallet for a medical convention. It doesn't make sense.'

'Neither does anything else,' Piper said.

'Except what you suggested days ago. Remember your idea that it could've been his wife he met?'

'Yes, but the same objection applies. Why meet there?'

'Let's worry about that later. Suppose he'd promised to phone her before he left the hospital and he forgot? Suppose he realized she might be anxious if she didn't hear from him and so he stopped at a call box?'

'All right . . . suppose. How would she persuade him to drive to the cliffs and wait for her? And he'd have to wait. He was part way to Dorchester when she was still in London. Have you thought of that?'

Quinn said, 'I've thought of everything. Now I'm right back where I started. The only answer is that he wanted to disappear and make it look as if he'd committed suicide.'

'For what reason?'

'Possibly because he was in a mess. He'd done something that a professional man shouldn't oughta done and he couldn't stand public humiliation.'

'But I don't believe he was the type of man who'd do such a thing. Neither does Dr Egan. Everybody has always had the highest opinion of Heseltine. You were told that yourself. He was respected by the staff and all his colleagues at the Brompton Clinic.'

'Except Stone, the ENT man,' Quinn said. 'And Mrs Heseltine seems to have been pretty quick to believe the worst of her husband.'

At the other end of the phone there was a long silence. Then Piper said doubtfully, 'I wouldn't pay too much attention to Stone. Chances are he and Heseltine have never got on well together. Could be little more than that.'

'What about Mrs H? On the one hand she has a guilt-complex and on the other she thinks her husband quite capable of cold-blooded murder. She wouldn't say a thing like that without good reason.'

Quinn hesitated for a moment before he added, 'Or bad reason. I'd still like to know where she was on Saturday between midday and midnight. However, do you mind if I ask you a personal question?'

'Any objection I might have wouldn't stop you.'

'Probably not. But you're not obliged to answer. The question is: would you back out of these inquiries if you felt they might land Mrs Heseltine in real trouble?'

Piper needed time for thought. At last, he said, 'I wouldn't be happy at the prospect . . . but I can't forget Heseltine's kindness to me when I'd just about reached the end of my tether. I feel it's my duty to find out what's happened to him.'

'Meaning that his wife comes second?'

'Yes, I'm afraid that's how it's got to be.'

'If you want my opinion, you've made the right choice,' Quinn said. 'I'm sure Lynn Heseltine knows more than she's willing to tell. In the meantime, I think I ought to ring the hospital and find out how old Mrs Gordon is getting on. Ta-ta for now . . .'

Ward sister was polite but non-committal. Although the patient had made satisfactory progress she was still too weak to receive visitors.

'. . . Are you a relative?'

'No, just somebody who feels kind of sorry for the old lass.'

'Well, I'd advise you to phone in a day or two. By that time we may be able to tell you when you can come and see her.'

'Thanks,' Quinn said. 'Wish her well for me.'

He skimmed through several of the dailies, noted a couple of items that might be worth following up and spent another ten minutes thinking over what Piper had told him about the fair-haired pretty girl who was a member of Stone's surgical team.

Part of her brief conversation with Piper repeated itself in Quinn's mind. There seemed no reason why it should have any special significance but it refused to leave him.

'. . . *Did you see him at all last Saturday?*'

'. . . *Only in passing. I had a day off and didn't have to come on duty until seven o'clock. Got here about a quarter to seven and saw Mr Heseltine driving away as I parked my car.*'

'*Was he alone?*'

'*Oh yes. I'm sure of that. There was no one else with him.*'

'*Anything unusual about him that you remember? I men, did he look ill or upset?*'

'. . . *Not that I noticed. Of course, I was a short distance away from him . . . but he seemed all right to me . . .*'

Christine Bowater had seen Heseltine. It seemed unimportant whether Heseltine had seen her. So many things were unimportant on the surface. Yet all the trivialities added up to the events of Saturday night when a man had parked his car, placed his jacket and cap on the edge of the cliff and then vanished like a spectre in the moonlight, someone who had never been.

Behind that childish thought followed another. Mrs Heseltine believed her husband had been involved with another woman . . . or that was what she said she believed. Perhaps she wanted to believe it . . . perhaps . . .

There were two conclusions which might be drawn from that train of thought. Neither answered the riddle of Robert Heseltine's disappearance . . . but one of them pointed the way to what might well be the answer.

Quinn scrawled some more doodles. Each was a copy of all the rest: a matchstick man behind the wheel of a car and above it a disc representing the moon.

He felt empty inside but he had no appetite. Most days

he would have gone to the Three Feathers by now for a sandwich and a pint of bitter but this was an odd day. The thought of beer repelled him.

Amongst the noisy bustle of the reporters' room he seemed isolated and alone. Everybody else was busily occupied, everybody else had a purpose to fulfil. Only he had no object in life.

It was one of those days. He knew it would pass . . . it always did. Most times a mood like this was the price he paid for a hangover. What he needed was something to buck him up.

So he went back to the canteen and had some toast and a mug of hot sweet tea. They helped but not very much. He was still in the wrong frame of mind for work, the wrong frame of mind for anything.

. . . One of those days. No one to blame but yourself. You didn't have to get a skinful last night. Trouble is you don't have the right sort of pals and you're easily led astray. Like the foolish virgin you can't say no . . .

He was on his way downstairs when somebody told him he was wanted on the phone. '. . . Couldn't say who. I didn't take the call. By the look of you, I'd say it's the crematorium to ask if you'd like an early reservation . . .'

The connection was bad and he could barely hear the voice at the other end. Then the line suddenly cleared.

It was Downey's voice. He said, 'Got news for you, Mr Quinn. Dorchester police have just received a message via the coastguard station at South Bay. It was from a cargo vessel heading for Sidmouth. Not much detail at the moment but I thought I'd let you know right away so you could – '

'Never mind the details,' Quinn said. 'What's the message?'

'Well, it seems the ship picked up a body two or three miles off-shore west of the cliffs near Little Mallet. The captain reports that he searched . . .'

There the line buzzed and crackled again. For a moment Quinn heard only a few disjointed words.

When the noise stopped, Downey was saying '. . . cheque book in one of the trouser pockets. The cuff-links bear a monogram RQH and the name printed on the cheques is Robert Q. Heseltine. Looks as if the law can give up searching for him now . . . doesn't it?'

CHAPTER XII

MRS HESELTINE travelled to Dorchester the following morning. By that time the body had been put ashore and taken to the town mortuary.

A post-mortem examination carried out late Thursday night had revealed that death was due to drowning. There was some bruising of the head which the pathologist considered was likely to have been caused when the deceased entered the water.

'. . . One bruise in particular was of a severe nature and would certainly have rendered him unconscious. I found damage to the brain substance which could have caused death by itself if drowning had not supervened. From information given to me I would say he was dashed against the rocks . . .'

Time since death occurred was estimated as between five and six days. No indications of any organic disease were found. Deceased was a man of approximately forty-five years of age, well-nourished and of good general physique.

At a quarter to twelve on Friday morning, Lynn Heseltine was taken to the mortuary where she identified the body as that of her husband, Robert Quentin Heseltine, whom she had last seen the previous Saturday, August 20. Interviewed subsequently by Detective-Superintendent Wainwright of Dorchester CID, she stated that she had no idea how her husband came to be in the water. As she had already informed the police when he was first reported missing, she could suggest no reason why he should wish to take his own life.

Quinn had a short discussion with his news editor before setting off for Dorchester on Friday afternoon. '. . . Inquest is being held tomorrow. I've a feeling it may be adjourned after cause of death and formal identification.'

'Then why bother going?'

'I want to see how Mrs Lynn Heseltine deports herself . . . as the Victorians would say. Interesting to watch what sort of weeping widow act she puts on.'

'Might not be an act. What have you got against her?'

'Nothing I could put into words.'

The news editor said, 'If you can't put it into words, it must be quite something. Mind how you go – that's all. And take it easy on the expense account. The paper's not made of money.'

'No, but –' Quinn showed his teeth like a horse – 'but money's made of paper. Don't you think I'm a real wag?'

'Only one thing about you that wags is your tongue. Like to do me a favour?'

'It'll cost you. What's the favour?'

'Go and take a walk on the cliffs at Little Mallet . . . with your eyes shut. Now – out. One of us has work to do.'

'You'll be sorry when I'm gone.'

'Correction.' The news editor pointed to the door. 'I'll only be sorry when you come back. Goodbye . . .'

Quinn left London in a borrowed staff car soon after two o'clock. He took the route he believed Robert Heseltine had taken on Saturday evening, August 20.

To Staines along the A316 . . . Bagshot via the A30 and on to the M3. Where the motorway ended he rejoined the A30.

Sutton Scotney . . . Stockbridge . . . Lopscombe Corner . . . Salisbury . . . the A354 to Blandford . . . then south-west. The sun was in his eyes most of the time now.

He reached Dorchester about five. On a sudden impulse he drove through the town without stopping.

As he followed the old Roman road he had an uneasy feeling that a dead man was sitting beside him. He could almost believe Robert Heseltine was showing him the way.

That other time it had been growing dark when the tan

Mercedes arrived at Winterbourne Abbas. The moon was high as it continued along the A35 for another few miles until it came to the road heading south towards the Channel.

Now there was bright sunshine and only an occasional cloud. Yet the presence of the dead felt very real.

Soon Quinn saw the signpost he was looking for: *COMPTON EAGLE – 2m.* There he swung left on to a twisting narrow road.

Compton Eagle was a score of houses lining a single street. Long Mallet lay in the shadow of tall trees, with leaves already losing their summer green. Beyond the village the road was hardly better than a farm track.

He caught only a glimpse of Little Mallet over to his left as he drove between overgrown hedges. Where the banks rose higher still he could see nothing at all and every corner became a hazard.

The road was now a rutted lane. Moments later it ended at a footpath running at right-angles close to the winding cliff top. He could see the waters of the Channel glistening in sunlight.

Just before he came to the footpath he stopped and got out. A fringe of scrub grass lined the edge of the cliff. Very slowly he walked across the verge until he could go no further. Then he stood looking down at the sea.

There were rocks at the foot of the cliff – tumbled rocks worn smooth by time and tide. As he watched, his mind filled with sombre thoughts, the waves climbed high and fell back . . . again . . . and again . . . and again.

This was where it had happened. This was where a man had plummeted down into the surging water and been hurled against one of those half-covered rocks. This was where he had come to his journey's end.

Why he had chosen this spot and whether he had met someone here were questions that might never be answered. But at least his fate was known. He was not just a man who had disappeared. The sea had given up its dead.

Now Lynn Heseltine need no longer fear a knock at the door or the ringing of the phone bell. Now she knew the worst. Now the thing she had been afraid of could be buried along with her husband.

Quinn wondered how she had felt when they took her into the mortuary – that place of death and disinfectant where the living walked on quiet feet and talked in quiet voices. Perhaps she had still clung to a vestige of hope even at the last moment.

'. . . *Is that your husband, Mrs Heseltine?*'

For any woman it would be a traumatic experience. He had been in the sea nearly five whole days. His swollen discoloured face would haunt her dreams for a long time to come.

Unless . . . the call of a seagull sounded loud in Quinn's head. It startled him into recognition of what he had been thinking.

Mrs Heseltine had identified her husband. Although he must have been a travesty of the man she had known, she had identified him. And on her identification, the body would be buried in Robert Heseltine's grave.

Why she should lie was a question that no one would ask. Who could have taken her husband's place was a question that Quinn was unable to answer.

A seagull swooped over the cliff top and floated on outspread wings high above the sea. Quinn watched it circle lazily down and land on one of the rocks.

Near where it was preening itself a man had died. To think that the man could have been anyone but Robert Heseltine was absurd. Yet, to think that Heseltine would take his own life was equally absurd.

The police might be able to help. They would know how closely the drowned man answered Heseltine's general description.

It cost nothing to ask. And Quinn told himself he had no need to explain why he was asking. Detective-Superintendent Wainwright could think what he liked.

He was a man of compact build, grizzled hair and slate-grey eyes. In manner and expression he could never have been taken for anything but a policeman.

When he had pulled forward a chair and gone back round to the other side of his desk, he said, 'You're lucky to catch me, Mr Quinn. I was just about to call it a day. You come all the way from London specially to see me?'

'Not exactly. My main purpose was to attend the inquest tomorrow morning.'

'Seems a long journey for very little. Didn't your man Downey tell you we're going to ask for an adjournment after identity and cause of death have been established?'

Quinn said, 'Yes, I gathered as much. But it gave me an excuse to come and take a look at the place where it all happened.'

'That's not –' Wainwright shook his head – 'not quite how I'd describe this sort of affair.'

'No? Then how would you describe it?'

'Not by saying it all happened when Heseltine jumped off the cliff. In my opinion that was merely the climax of a series of events. You'd probably have to go back a long way to find the motive.'

'Wouldn't get you anywhere if you did,' Quinn said.

'Seldom does. From what I've read there are about as many motives for suicide as there are suicides.'

'True enough. But that's the trouble in this case. No one's been able to suggest any motive.'

With a sharper look in his eyes, Wainwright asked, 'Are you suggesting it wasn't suicide?'

'No, I wouldn't go as far as that. The thing is it's not every day that a well-known surgeon like Robert Q. Heseltine goes for a swim with his clothes on. And my column thrives on background material. Here I can't find any that's relevant.'

'Sorry.' The superintendent shook his head again. 'Afraid

I can't help you. If there's nothing else . . .'

'Well, if you can spare the time, you could help me.'

'How?'

'By letting me have a list of the things you found on Heseltine's body. Also what was in the pockets of his linen jacket and in his car.'

Wainwright shrugged. He said, 'Don't see where that'll get you but the information isn't secret. You can have it with pleasure.'

He opened a drawer in his desk and brought out a folder. When he had turned over a number of papers, he read out : 'On the body, the following – a wristwatch; a leather key-case; a handkerchief; a pair of monogrammed cuff-links; a cheque book; some small change. Got that?'

'Six items,' Quinn said. 'Apart from the watch and the cuff-links, I presume the rest were in his trouser pockets?'

'That's right. Now for the linen jacket : a wallet containing £57 in five-pound and one-pound notes; a book of postage stamps; some visiting cards; a comb; an AA member's wallet containing a car insurance certificate, a membership certificate, a driving licence and a bank card. That's the lot.'

'What about his car?'

'Oh, I'll give you that too. There were various maps and guide books in the glove compartments along with some literature distributed by drug houses, a London street directory, an aerosol can of the stuff for cleaning windscreens and two pairs of gloves – one leather, the other pair cotton?'

'Nothing else?'

'Only a soiled duster and an opened packet of paper handkerchiefs. What else did you think there should be?'

Quinn had a fleeting idea that vanished before he could put a name to it. He was still trying to bring it back as he said, 'I don't know. Most cars have a lot of junk lying around.'

'Well, the late Mr Heseltine was a tidy customer. He hadn't littered his car with junk. Might've done in time, of course, but the Mercedes was only three months old.'

Superintendent Wainwright turned over another sheet of paper, glanced up and asked, 'Want to know the contents of his medical bag?'

'Not if they were just the usual things you'd expect to find.'

'My experience is limited. But our police surgeon inspected it and he told me it contained the usual equipment.'

'That leaves the overnight case,' Quinn said.

'Yes, it's all here. An electric razor, toothbrush, tube of toothpaste, pair of pyjamas, dressing-gown, slippers, two pairs of socks, four handkerchiefs, a couple of ties, two newly-laundered shirts in their cellophane wrappers, talcum powder, a flask of pre-shave lotion, a tube of hair cream, a comb, a set of underwear and a coat hanger.'

'The complete traveller,' Quinn said.

'So it would appear. Can you suggest anything he left out?'

'No, not really.' That fleeting idea came and went again without shape or form. 'He seems to have taken more than enough for a one-night stay.'

'And didn't use –' Wainwright straightened himself and cleared his throat – 'any of it. Strange affair from any angle.'

'You can say that again.'

'Wonder whether it would've made any difference to the outcome if he hadn't been asked by his aunt's doctor to come and take a look at her?'

Quinn said, 'Good question. Didn't show much consideration for the lady, did he?'

'Don't suppose he was in the mood to consider anybody but himself.'

'Are you saying what he did was selfish?'

'Suicide is the ultimate selfishness,' Wainwright said.

'I like that phrase.' Quinn put his notebook in his pocket and stood up. 'Must remember to use it some time. For that and also your patience with an earnest seeker after the truth, my thanks, Superintendent. Could you recommend a hotel where I might lay my weary head?'

Wainwright said, 'Try the Imperial. It's one of the best hotels in town.'

'Good. Know any decent pubs?'

'Well, the Ram's Horn sells a nice glass of beer. Owned by a small independent brewery that's been in the family for generations. You'll find the place –'

'By following my nose,' Quinn said. 'And thanks again. If I'd had no other reason for coming to Dorchester, my journey would not have been in vain. It'll be a change to quaff ale that hasn't been brewed from an accountant's recipe. See you in the morning . . .'

When he had booked in at the Imperial he parked his car and went to his room. After he had freshened up he ate his first meal of the day. Then someone directed him to the Ram's Horn.

It lived up to its reputation. He enjoyed the beer; the lack of juke-box and modern fittings; the warmth of the small-town atmosphere. Most of all, he relished complete anonymity.

No one knew him. No one wanted to involve him in pub conversation. For an hour or two he had the chance to think without distraction.

Thinking and drinking never went well together so he made a couple of pints last until it was time for bed. He wanted an early night . . . and it would do no good to sour his stomach again.

. . . You had more than your quota last night. Need a clear head tomorrow. Wonder if Mrs Heseltine is staying at the same hotel? Maybe she's been put up by her late husband's aunt. Bound to have gone to see her. Hard lines on the old lass. Whatever she's suffering from, the news won't have done her any good . . .

It was barely ten o'clock when he got back to his hotel.

As he undressed he went on thinking about another man who had come to Dorchester on another night.

He, too, had driven through the town and taken the road that led past Little Mallet. But he had not returned.

Tomorrow an inquest would decide who he had been and how he had died. There was scarcely any doubt what the verdict would be . . . and not much doubt that it was the right verdict. Yet . . .

After he had switched off the lights and drawn back the curtains, Quinn stood for a while looking out at the moon. Same moon as on that other night but now with a segment cut out of the eastern side.

Almost the same time, as well. Heseltine's car had passed a woman called Rose Lofthouse between half past nine and a quarter to ten. By this time last Saturday night, Robert Heseltine had been dead.

All the things he needed for his stay in Dorchester were in those two bags. It was silly to question what he had intended to do when he left London. But he had changed his mind . . . or events had changed it for him.

As Quinn climbed into bed the fugitive idea taunted him once more. Now it was accompanied by the echo of Superintendent Wainwright's voice asking '. . . *What else did you think there should be?*'

The question repeated itself again and again. It was still unanswered as Quinn drifted off to sleep.

But one thing he knew beyond question. The list of Heseltine's possessions was incomplete. Something was missing . . . something was missing . . .

CHAPTER XIII

THE INQUEST PROCEEDINGS were reduced to the barest minimum. From start to finish they lasted little more than twenty minutes.

A deposition from the captain of the cargo vessel *Sarah Lee* was read out by the coroner. It stated that the body of a man had been taken from the sea five miles WSW of Ashcombe at 1033 hours Thursday, August 25.

'. . . He was wearing shoes, socks, underwear, trousers of the hip-fitting type, shirt, tie, cuff-links and a wrist-watch. The contents of his trouser pockets are separately listed. I estimate he had been in the water several days. Documents found on him gave his name at Robert Q. Heseltine of Martendale Crescent, Canon's Park, London . . .'

Then followed an account of steps taken by the captain of the *Sarah Lee* to have the body put ashore, after he had sent a radio message to the nearest coastguard station. The deposition had been sworn before a notary public.

Detective-Superintendent Wainwright gave evidence that he had taken charge of the body on Thursday evening, August 25. He confirmed the list of items found on the deceased.

A pathologist described his findings at a post-mortem examination. He stated that there was some injury to the head and gave his opinion as to how this had been caused.

One injury in particular might well have had fatal results in other circumstances. Death, however, had been due to **drowning.**

'. . . Taking all relevant factors into consideration, I would say he had died five or six days prior to my examination.'

'That would be either Saturday the twentieth or Sunday the twenty-first of August?'

'As closely as it is possible to estimate, sir.'

A Mrs Rose Lofthouse told the coroner what she had seen on the night of August twentieth. She was a shapeless woman with masculine features and skimpy hair. Quinn thought she would hardly need a dog for protection when she took a walk at night.

'. . . If I hadn't got well into the hedge he'd have run me over. Close enough for me to get a good look at him but he didn't seem to have seen me.'

'Was there anything in his appearance that might be described as unusual?'

'Well, the peak of his cap threw a shadow over his eyes but I had a feeling he was staring straight in front of him. No expression on his face, either. The only way I can put it is that he had a kind of dead look.'

'Have you ever seen anyone look like that before, Mrs Lofthouse?'

'Yes, once. A man who'd been drinking got on the bus. I was reminded of him when I thought about the driver of the car that nearly knocked me down.'

'Was the car being driven erratically?'

'No . . . a bit too fast for such a narrow road but I wouldn't have thought anything of it if he hadn't made me get out of his way in a hurry. I still feel he should have stopped whatever happened.'

'What time did this take place?'

'Between half past nine and a quarter to ten . . . as near as I can say.'

'Did the car have its headlights on?'

'Yes, but even without them he couldn't miss seeing me.

There was a full moon that made things almost as light as day . . .'

The pathologist was recalled. When asked if the deceased could have been suffering from the effects of drink, he said, 'I would not care to be too definite in my opinion, sir. Difficulty in cases of drowning arises when some length of time elapses before the body is recovered.'

'Perhaps, for the benefit of the jury, you would explain the nature of this difficulty?'

'By all means. After putrefaction is established, the chemistry of the blood becomes disturbed by organic changes. In some instances it may prove impossible even to show the exact cause of death. The presence of alcohol in the bloodstream may not always yield to analysis.'

The coroner said, 'I see. But you are satisfied that, in this case, death was due to drowning?'

'That is my considered opinion, sir.'

Mrs Lynn Heseltine was last to be called. As she took her place in the witness box she looked tired but very beautiful – a slim, elegant woman with perfect grooming.

It was in her eyes that weariness lay like a shadow. Quinn would have wagered she had slept very little if at all.

She answered the coroner's questions in a low subdued voice. Once or twice she had to repeat her answers.

Yes, she had visited the mortuary and there shown the body of a man who, she understood, had been picked up in the English Channel. It was her husband Robert Heseltine.

'You were able to make a positive identification?'

Her lips trembled. Almost inaudibly, she said, 'Yes. I'm quite sure.'

'Did you inspect various articles that had been in his pockets?'

'They showed me a leather key-case and a cheque book. I recognized them as well as his wristwatch and cuff-links.

All of them belonged to my husband.'

The coroner said, 'Thank you, Mrs Heseltine. I have no
wish to prolong what must be a painful ordeal for you. That
will be all.'

After a few formalities had been concluded he issued a
burial certificate. Then, on the application of the police,
the inquest was adjourned for fourteen days.

When they left the courtroom, Downey asked, 'Well,
where do you go from here?'

He was a tall young man with an old man's fuzzy beard.
From the moment they met he had treated Quinn with
marked respect.

Quinn said, 'I'm going to a pub called the Ram's Horn.
And you're coming with me. What's more, you'll buy me a
pint of vintage bitter. Right?'

In a bright voice, Downey said, 'It'll be my pleasure . . .'

As they walked through the morning sunshine, he added,
'Don't suppose I'll get much chance of having a drink with
you after this. You won't be back in these parts for a while.'

'I haven't gone yet,' Quinn said. 'Heseltine may be dead
but the story isn't.'

'How do you make that out?'

'Something doesn't add up right – that's how. There's a
bit missing.'

'What bit?'

'If I knew that, I'd be a clever boy. It's like the conjur-
ing trick: now you see it, now you don't. And right now, I
don't.'

Downey said, 'Can't help you, I'm afraid. It's 'way beyond me. I'd thought the whole thing was over and done
with.'

They walked on, Quinn with his raincoat unbuttoned
and his hands in his trouser pockets. He hated to admit it
even to himself but this trip to Dorchester was beginning
to look like a waste of time.

Nothing new had come out at the inquest and he had

achieved very little by visiting the cliff top where Heseltine had abandoned his car and left his jacket and cap. The place was just as Downey had described it. And he could have approached Detective-Superintendent Wainwright for the list of Heseltine's possessions.

... *Either the body they fished out of the Channel is Robert Heseltine or it isn't. If it isn't, then Mrs Heseltine's a liar. No chance that she could be making an honest mistake. Her identification was positive. What's more, the corpse was wearing Heseltine's wristwatch and cuff-links. So, if it is somebody else, the answer is obvious* . . .

Motive was the problem – motive for the whole affair right from the very start. Everything fitted just too completely when it could not logically be complete. The motive was missing. And, even if that were ignored, there was something else of greater importance.

What it was still eluded him. He would know it if he saw it . . . but it never stayed long enough in one place. And always he ran the risk that he might be wrong. The missing piece might have no real significance . . .

Perhaps Downey read his mood. They walked the rest of the way in silence.

When they got to the Ram's Horn it had only just opened. There were very few customers in the lounge bar and they had no trouble finding a couple of stools at the quieter end.

They were served by a small plump barmaid with flaxen plaits that hung in front of her. She brought two pints of bitter, thanked Downey nicely when he told her to keep the change, and went off to attend to another customer.

He raised his glass and said, 'Cheers, Mr Quinn, and success to your endeavours. I don't know what you're looking for but I hope you find it.'

Quinn said, 'As the bishop said to the actress . . . I forgot to ask your pal Wainwright yesterday if he had a general description of Robert Heseltine. Would you know?'

'Oh yes. He got it from Mrs Heseltine through the local

police at Canon's Park last Sunday. Also a photograph.'

'So there can't be much doubt the dead man is Heseltine?'

'None at all.' Downey put down his glass. 'Have you some idea it might not be?'

'Just a passing notion.'

'You must be joking.'

'That fellow who was picked up by the *Sarah Lee* will tell you it's no joke.'

'But it must be Robert Heseltine. Apart from the description and the photograph that the police have, he was identified by his wife.'

'Who provided the description,' Quinn said. 'And the picture of a live man isn't a good likeness of a dead one who's been in the sea five days.'

After he had stood tugging at his beard for a while, Downey asked, 'If it isn't Heseltine who is it?'

'Your guess is as good as mine. Furthermore, let me ask the questions. You can supply the answers.'

'But I haven't any. Certainly none on those lines.'

'Me, neither. That's why I told you the story isn't dead yet.'

Downey stared down into his glass. When he looked up, he said, 'I've a feeling you know more than you've let on.'

'All I know is that I'm not satisfied. A nagging doubt won't let me believe what everybody else is willing to believe. Maybe they're right. Maybe I'm crazy.'

'That'll be the day,' Downey said.

'Your sublime faith is very touching.' Quinn took a long drink, smacked his lips and took another. 'Nectar of the gods, that's what this is. You can't buy ale like it anywhere in London.'

'Then drink up – ' Downey beckoned to the flaxen-haired barmaid – 'and have another.'

'Are you joining me?'

'Of course. I intend to look after you while you're here.'

'Good. But it's my shout.'

'Nonsense, Mr Quinn. As a visitor to the town you're my guest. Any time I come up to London you can reciprocate.'

'Sounds a trifle vulgar but I'll try anything once,' Quinn said.

At half past two they left the Ram's Horn in a mood of mellow friendship. Downey arranged to phone in the story of the inquest proceedings. Quinn returned to his hotel in time to get a late lunch.

Then he went upstairs, took off his shoes and lay down on the bed. The room was warm in the afternoon sunshine. For an hour he thought . . . and dozed off . . . and awoke to think again.

When at last he fell into a deeper sleep it was the sun on his face that wakened him. And as he rolled over an image took shape in his mind. This time it was sharp and clear. This time he recognized it. Now he knew he had been right when he guessed that something was missing.

There could be a reason why it had never been mentioned. Perhaps no one had thought of it. That might well be the explanation. And there had to be one. Something that had once existed could not just cease to exist.

He got up off the bed, bathed his face in cold water and paced the floor from wall to wall, again and again and again. What he had stumbled on might be explained away quite simply. Until he knew his guess had real substance it would be stupid to throw his hat in the air.

. . . *Assuming you had a hat. Open a big mouth too soon and they'll say it's a bonnet and you've got a bee in it. As Mrs Buchanan would say: Facts are chiels that winna ding. So you'd better make sure it is a fact. Cost you nothing to take another look . . .*

It was a quarter past five when he went downstairs and collected his car from the hotel garage. By five-thirty he was within sight of Winterbourne Abbas.

Through his open window the air was warm and dusty as he turned off the main road west and headed for Comp-

ton Eagle. Soon he was beyond the village . . . through
Long Mallet . . . glimpsing Little Mallet on his left as he
drove along the rutted lane that pointed south.

He could smell the sea. Ahead of him the sky was lumin-
ous with the reflection of sunlit waters. It seemed too peaceful a place for what had happened the night Robert Heseltine came this way under the light of the moon.

If he had arrived before nightfall many things would
have been different. It might be that the cargo vessel *Sarah
Lee* would not have had to interrupt her voyage to take the
body of a drowned man ashore.

Facts are chiels that winna ding . . . The only facts were
that a man called Robert Q. Heseltine had disappeared on
Saturday night, August 20: a man answering Heseltine's
description had been fished out of the sea on Thursday,
August 25: on Saturday, August 27, a jury had accepted
the drowned man's identity and a burial certificate had
been issued so that his body might be legally disposed of.

Those were the facts. Nothing else was known for certain. As Quinn pulled up at the place where he had
stopped the previous day, he told himself all the rest was
conjecture.

Then he began his search. Like a hunting-dog he quar-
tered both sides of the path winding parallel to the cliff
edge, concentrating eventually on the stretch of coarse
grass all around the spot where Heseltine's cap and linen
jacket had been found.

To be done thoroughly it was a lengthy task. And Quinn
had made up his mind before he started that he would be
thorough. If he failed it had to be for one reason only:
what he was searching for was not there.

That would mean it had never been there. If so, a new
concept had to be reckoned with.

. . . *Everybody will have been wrong except oor Wullie
. . . as Mrs B would say. It's asking a lot. Maybe I'm
kidding myself. But I've got to try* . . .

He went on trying for a long time. Again and again he

crossed and re-crossed the winding path, searching every square foot of the area, picking up and discarding scraps of paper, a crumpled ice-cream carton, pieces of broken glass, a plastic cup minus its handle . . . all the discarded refuse of a hundred summer picnics.

In the end he had to admit failure. By ten past six his back was aching and he had nothing to show for his labour — nothing tangible.

But a negative result was often proof in itself. Now the search would have to be widened.

. . . You can do no more here. Your next step is to question someone you've never met . . . and ask her a question she's already answered. This time she may give a different answer. It has to be . . . it just has to be . . .

He drove back to Dorchester, phoned Downey from the Imperial and told him there had been a change of plan. '. . . I've got an urgent job to do in the Big City. With regret I must take my leave of your very hospitable town. Hope you and I get together again some time. I enjoyed today's session in the Ram's Horn . . .'

It began to rain as he was approaching London. By the time he returned his car to the staff garage the rain had become a steady downpour.

With his coat collar turned up and his hands deep in his pockets he trotted to the nearest phone box. It was then not far off ten o'clock.

While he listened to the bell ringing out at the other end of the line he was thinking of a man who had died almost exactly one week ago — a man who had made this same journey in reverse. The waters of the English Channel had awaited him. By ten o'clock his problems were over.

Rain lashed against the door of the phone box and went rushing along the street. Quinn felt a touch of sadness as he pictured those last moments when a man had gone to his lonely death under the moon. It seemed wrong that there should have been no one with him to offer the final comfort of regret.

Yet death was always lonely. All men were alone when the end came. The only difference with him was that his ultimate journey had begun while he was still alive.

Another gust of rain swept the pavement. Then the phone said, 'Brompton Clinic.'

Quinn shook off his mood of depression. He said, 'I'd like to speak to Dr Bowater, please.'

'One moment. I'll see if she's available . . .'

He had to wait fully a minute before the operator said, 'Dr Bowater isn't on duty tonight. She's off until tomorrow afternoon.'

'In that case, could you give me her telephone number at home?'

'I'm not sure I can. Are you a patient?'

'No, this is a personal matter. Nothing to do with the hospital.'

Bolstering the truth with a small lie gave Quinn no twinge of conscience as he added, 'I've mislaid her phone number or I wouldn't need to trouble you.'

'Oh, I see. Very well . . .'

He repeated the number, told the operator he was grateful and hung up. Then he felt in his pocket for some more small change.

Christine Bowater's phone rang for a long time without answer. He told himself there was no reason why she should not be out for the evening . . . or spending the night with a friend.

Girl-friend or boy-friend . . . It was none of his business. All he wanted from her was a simple answer to a simple question. She could hardly refuse. If she did . . . He would cross that bridge when he came to it.

The *burr-burr . . . burr-burr . . . burr-burr* stopped. A woman's voice asked, 'Hello? Who is that?'

He said, 'My name's Quinn – Q-U-I-N-N. I believe

you've met a friend of mine, John Piper?'

'Yes, I have.' She sounded less than friendly when she asked, 'What is it you want?'

'Just a word with you about last Saturday evening when you arrived at the hospital to go on duty.'

'I don't understand. Why should I discuss a thing like that with you?'

'There's nothing secret about it,' Quinn said. 'I'd just like you to think back and –'

'At this hour of the night I've no intention of letting myself be interrogated by a stranger. Do you know what time it is?'

'Not much after ten. And it'll only take a minute.'

In a hostile voice, she said, 'I don't care how long it'll take. There's a proper time for everything. You can speak to me tomorrow morning – not right now.'

'OK. Sorry if I've annoyed you. What time do you want me to ring?'

'Between eleven and twelve o'clock. And I only hope it's important.'

'Oh, you can rest assured of that,' Quinn said. 'Mind telling me where you live?'

She told him that was no concern of his. '. . . I must say that Mr Piper has some very peculiar friends.'

Quinn said, 'I'm the only peculiar one. My apologies for disturbing you. I'll phone in the morning . . .'

CHAPTER XIV

Mrs Buchanan must have heard him unlocking the front door. She came out of the kitchen as he was about to take off his dripping raincoat.

In a tone of reproof, she said, 'Ye look as if ye'd fell in the river. I thought ye telt me ye'd be awa' for the weekend?'

'Man proposes,' Quinn said. 'The way things turned out I had to come back. And to prove it, I'm here.'

'I can see that for masel'. If ye stand there blethering ye'll soak ma lobby corpet. Gie me yer coat and Ah'll hang it up afore the kitchen fire. Then Ah'll mak ye some hot cocoa to put warmth in yer bones. Ye look hauf starved.'

Her eyes denied the gruffness in her voice. Quinn said, 'I am . . . both with cold and with hunger. A bite to eat as well as the cocoa would be very welcome.'

'Ye hae nae need tae remind me o' mah duties. Has there ever been a day when I havnae asked ye tae sit yersel' doon tae a guid meal and is it no' a fact ye're aye saying ye've nae appetite?'

Quinn said, 'There hasn't . . . and it is. Now I've got one big enough to eat you out of house and home.'

'It's no' afore time. Come awa' ben the kitchen and Ah'll mak ye something in twa shakes. The way ye neglect yersel' is a proper scandal. Whit wi' drinking and gallivanting until a' oors it's a wonder hoo ye keep body and soul thegether . . .'

She went on grumbling while she set the table and prepared a quick meal. He listened with only half a mind as he dried himself in front of the fire with a hand towel that she brought from a cupboard of sweet-smelling linen.

His thoughts were still on a girl called Christine Bowater. She had taken a long time to answer the phone.

When she did answer it, her manner could only be described as rude.

Ten o'clock was by no means late for receiving a phone call. Yet she had sounded as if he were intruding on something important. While he towelled his hair he wondered about that.

Maybe she had been taking a bath. Maybe she had been in bed and there was no phone at the bedside.

She could hardly have been asleep at that hour. And it would not be such a hardship to get out of bed – certainly not enough to justify the way she had spoken to him.

He let his ideas wander. Perhaps it was wrong of him to wonder if his call had come at an awkward moment. Perhaps Dr Bowater had been impatient to the point of rudeness because he had interrupted something. He could guess what that might have been. His guess would also explain her delay in answering the phone.

Still, it was her own business. No one had any right to cast reflections on her private life.

. . . For all you know, she may be married. It's not the only thing you don't know about her. And it doesn't really matter whether she's married, single, widowed or divorced. What counts is her answer to that one question if you can persuade her to think it over . . .

Mrs Buchanan was talking to him, hands on hips, her face peevish. '. . . How mony times have ye tae be telt tae sit yersel' doon? Ye were supposed to be fair famished.'

'I'm sorry,' Quinn said. 'I didn't hear you.'

As he sat down at the table, he added, 'That looks real good, Mrs B. I think I'll take your advice and get wed. May I have your hand in marriage?'

'Ye'll hae mah hand roon yer ear if Ah hae ony mair cheek. Soon as ye've pit that inside ye, get yersel' awa' tae bed.'

She left him alone after that. When he had finished his meal he went upstairs without seeing her again.

The sound of the rain made bed an inviting prospect. It was a long time since he had felt so tired. He undressed and slid between the sheets with an unusual sense of relief.

Then from far out of the past he remembered a line that took him back to his childhood: *The day Thou gavest, Lord, is ended . . .'*

On Saturday, August 20, a man called Robert Heseltine had not known that this was to be his last day. No one else had known, either. Perhaps it was better that way. Perhaps if a man could see what lay ahead . . .

Drowsy thoughts gathered in Quinn's mind. Voices were talking to him across the threshold of sleep. One voice remained when all the rest had drifted off into the darkness.

'. . . *Let's start with blackmail. It's as good a place as any.'*

That had been on Sunday morning when, for many people, it all began. Now another Sunday was almost here.

The news editor had been guessing. But it was a good guess. The only fault was that he might have got it wrong way round . . .

Quinn slept better than he had slept for weeks. When he woke just before seven o'clock his mind was refreshed and wide-awake.

The rain had stopped but the streets were still wet. From his bedroom window he looked out at a sky of shining blue, washed clean by the downpour that must have lasted most of the night.

By the time he went downstairs he had arranged his priorities for the day. Much depended on what Dr Christine Bowater might be able to tell him. But almost equally important could be the information he hoped to get about Robert Heseltine's aunt, Mrs Lloyd.

Maybe Piper could help there . . . if Piper had not made plans to go off somewhere for the day with Jane. If she were away from home he might be joining her. Quinn hoped she was away. It would avoid talking to her and getting another invitation to visit them.

'. . . *Why don't you have a meal with us one of these nights? It's a long time since we've seen you* . . .'

Everything was quiet downstairs. The table had been laid for breakfast: a jar of marmalade; coffee in the percolator; a plate and a cup and saucer; the electric toaster plugged in; several slices of bread under a damp tea cloth.

Sunday was Mrs Buchanan's morning for what she called a lie in. He made himself some toast and coffee, washed up after he had eaten and went out on tip-toe, closing the front door with barely a sound. As he set off on his regular walk to King's Cross underground he was feeling in his raincoat pockets for the cigarette that was never there.

Eight-twenty he arrived at Holborn. When he came out of the station, he walked at a leisurely pace to Fleet Street and sauntered the rest of the way, glancing in shop windows and enjoying the fresh air that smelled reasonably clean only one morning in the week.

Even though he tried to kill time he got to the office earlier than he could ever remember. There was no one in the reporters' room. When he went up to the library he found that Toby had not yet arrived. Quinn told himself he would have to rely on his own efforts for the information he wanted.

Among a stack of reference books he found a current diary with pages of astronomical material. One page tabulated the times of sunrise and sunset, week by week, in London; Newcastle; Norwich; Plymouth.

Calculated along the lines of latitude, the total distance between London and Plymouth was approximately 180 miles: the distance from Dorchester to Plymouth about three-sevenths of the total. Sunset in London on Saturday, August 20 had been 8.35 pm; in Plymouth on the same date, 8.30 pm. Three-sevenths of the difference . . .

There Quinn told himself he had no need for all this fancy calculation. Two or three minutes either way could not possibly matter.

. . . *Robert Heseltine must have passed through Dorchester that night at roughly 9.30. Sunset would've been, as near as dammit, 8.30. So, an hour after sunset, it must've been dark except for the light of the moon. Even travelling westward, sunlight would have long gone by the time he got to Winterbourne Abbas . . .*

A woman called Rose Lofthouse had seen the tan Mercedes south of Little Mallet between half past nine and a quarter to ten. At the inquest she had described precisely what she saw that night by the light of the moon.

By the light of the moon . . . It was like a phrase from an old song. Quinn wondered if he were crazy to imagine he was the only one to think of it. Might be a good idea to try it out on Piper.

. . . *Can't disturb him at this hour on a Sunday morning. It isn't nine o'clock yet. Plenty of time. You're not supposed to ring Dr Bowater before eleven. Don't hope for too much from her. If she's anything like her boss she'll probably not even give you a good morning . . .*

He felt dry. Something hot and sweet was indicated but the canteen would not be open until ten. So he went out and walked around and eventually found a Wimpy bar where he had two cups of coffee.

When he got back to the office it was well after nine and the place had come alive. Someone called out to him before he reached his desk.

'. . . Got a message for you. I told them you weren't likely to be in before the crack of high noon and they asked me to pass on the news soon's I saw you.'

'What news?'

'Sounds just up your street. A woman's been found dead in bed this morning. Carbon copy of that case you were on the other day – the one who cut her wrist. Seems this wench did the same thing. Your literary style must exert a powerful influence.'

'Granted. But I've got other things to do this morning. Give it to somebody else.'

'As you wish. All the same, I felt you'd be interested.'

'Nice of you to consider my interests. Now if there isn't –'

'You'd have thought she'd know easier ways of solving whatever her problems may have been.'

Something in the remark roused a sudden response in Quinn's mind. He asked, 'Why should she know easier ways?'

'Because she was a medic. Worked on one of the surgical teams at the Brompton Clinic. Her name was Bowater – Dr Christine Bowater. By the look on your aristocratic countenance I'd say it rings a bell.'

'You'd be right,' Quinn said.

The press officer at New Scotland Yard had very little additional information. It was too soon to make any further statement.

'. . . You'll have to wait for the results of the PM. You ought to know that.'

'A post-mortem will only confirm what the police surgeon must already have seen for himself. She wasn't shot, hanged or poisoned. Either she bled to death from a cut wrist or she didn't. The only question is whether she did the job or somebody else did it. What does it look like?'

'I wouldn't know. I wasn't there. All I'm paid to do is give out information that's given to me.'

'Money for old rope,' Quinn said.

'Opinions differ. And if you go on talking like that, next time I won't even tell you I haven't anything to tell you. There's another thing . . .'

'Yes?'

'You hinted that it might not have been self-inflicted.

What makes you think she didn't commit suicide?'

Quinn said, 'For the answer to that, I suggest you speak to my press officer.'

The news editor listened, his bulbous eyes half-shut, one hand beating time on the desk to a tune in his head. He never looked up once.

It was a short meeting. Quinn gave him only an account of the inquest at Dorchester and the news item that had just come in.

'. . . Can hardly be a coincidence that two women who were known to Robert Heseltine both died the same way.'

'Coincidence may not enter into it. The second one could've copied the method used in the first.'

'If the second one was suicide. It seems a strange way for a doctor to take her own life.'

'I wouldn't concentrate as much on that as on motive,' the news editor said.

'Hunting for motives hasn't got us anywhere so far. On the surface, Heseltine doesn't appear to have had one.'

'You'll have to dig below the surface. About time you came up with some kind of explanation. You've been at the centre of this affair right from the start. You know as much as anybody does and more than most. All you have to do is stay sober and use your head.'

'Yes, sir . . . very good, sir . . . three bags full, sir. For your information I'd arranged to phone Christine Bowater this morning and ask her a very particular question.'

'Such as?'

'Won't do any good to tell you. She can't answer it now.'

'Then find somebody else who can.'

Quinn said, 'What niggles me is that it shouldn't be necessary. I've got a feeling I know the answer.'

'You'll need to translate your feeling into fact before you have a story.'

'Sure. I'm convinced that Heseltine's aunt, Mrs Lloyd,

and her GP are linked with everything that's happened.'

The news editor said, 'Are you really? I'll soon be convinced you're losing your faculties. Of course his aunt and her doctor are linked with the whole business. They were his reason for going to Dorchester. Or have you forgotten?'

'That's not what I meant. But I can't explain. I only know that the road Heseltine followed on his last journey began at the hospital. Now death has travelled back along that same road to where the pattern of events was formed.'

'I asked for –' the news editor used his ballpen as a pointer – 'for facts and you give me frills. Save the fancy prose for your column.'

'One of these days I'll make you eat those words,' Quinn said. 'Meantime, think over what I've told you. Maybe it was the same road for the same reason.'

'Now you're being cryptic. I can stand anything but that.'

'There's nothing cryptic in what I'm telling you. Maybe Christine Bowater knew why the man they believe was Heseltine drowned in the English Channel. Maybe she shared the secret behind Heseltine's trip to the cliffs south of Little Mallet.'

The news editor asked, 'So what was this secret?'

'I don't know yet. But I've given you the key.'

'If you have, I must be mentally blind. Let's hear it again.'

'No need. It's nearly all in the suggestion you once made that blackmail might explain Heseltine's disappearance. Remember?'

'Yes. But if he were being blackmailed –'

'Don't be in such a hurry. It's the right key but you're trying to open the wrong door.'

'OK. Now I give up.'

'Only because you want it served up on a plate,' Quinn said. 'You forget that the end and the beginning may be one. It's like the Egyptian symbol of existence – a snake with its tail in its mouth . . .'

Piper answered the phone before it had rung three or four times. He said he had just finished reading about the inquest at Dorchester.

'. . . Any idea why the police wanted an adjournment?'

'Maybe they want to be quite sure it's Heseltine who was fished out of the sea,' Quinn said.

'Why should there be any doubt? His wife identified the body, didn't she?'

'Oh yes. But she could be mistaken. A man's appearance changes for the worse when he's been pickled in salt water for best part of a week.'

'Did she give the impression she wasn't too sure?'

'Far from it. The way she spoke at the inquest, I'd say it's Heseltine's body, all right . . . or she wants people to think it is.'

'That's a peculiar attitude to adopt,' Piper said. 'What possible motive could she have for lying?'

'I don't know . . . same as I don't know what possible motive her husband could've had for committing suicide. You've known the man a long time and you haven't been able to think of one.'

'By the same token, I can't imagine why Lynn Heseltine should suddenly become a liar.'

'Maybe it isn't such a sudden fall from grace,' Quinn said.

After a long silence, Piper asked, 'Is there something positive behind that insinuation?'

'No . . . just a hunch. And a vague one, at that. All the same, I think we've been looking at this affair the wrong way round.'

'How?'

'Everybody assumed it was a case of an erring husband. Suppose it was Lynn who'd strayed off the straight and narrow? Might that not explain her air of guilt that you detected?'

'But it wouldn't – '

Piper broke off. It took him quite a while to sort out his tangled thoughts.

Then he said, 'Even if you're right, it doesn't explain what happened on the cliffs at Little Mallet.'

'It might,' Quinn said.

'I don't see how. You're not going back to my silly notion that she might've been responsible for the events of last Saturday night . . . are you?'

'Not in the sense you meant. But let's say Heseltine left London at a quarter to seven. The journey shouldn't have taken three hours . . . so he must've stopped somewhere on the way.'

'There's no must. However, it's possible. But we've been all through that several times and we don't – '

'Not so fast. It was a warm sunny evening when he drove away from the Brompton Clinic. By sunset he'd have been on the road almost two hours. But – and it's a big but – it would be quite dark before he got anywhere near Little Mallet. Are you with me?'

'No. I haven't the faintest idea what you're talking about.'

'That's because you haven't had the advantage of a chat with Detective-Superintendent Wainwright. Nice fellow. Very co-operative.'

'Never mind his personality. What did he tell you?'

'Ah, that's where we get down to the nitty-gritty . . . if I may borrow a loathsome expression used by economists, politicians, union spokesmen and commentators on TV. The things they do to the English language would make Shakespeare – '

'I'm not interested in Shakespeare. What did Wainwright tell you?'

'Well, now, that's the whole point,' Quinn said. 'It's what he didn't tell me. There was something omitted.'

'Am I supposed to make sense out of that?'

'No, perhaps not. But I hope you can make sense out of

something that was phoned in about an hour ago. Remember the pretty girl you met when you visited the Brompton Clinic?'

'Yes, Christine Bowater. Dr Egan introduced us. What about her?'

'Nothing much. Only that she isn't a pretty girl any longer. She was found in bed with her wrist cut some time early this morning.'

In a shocked voice, Piper asked, 'Why should she want to kill herself? What on earth could make her do a thing like that?'

Quinn said, 'The information I've got is still incomplete. We don't know that she did . . . although it sounds like a repeat of the Pauline Gordon suicide.'

'Are you suggesting that Dr Bowater might not have taken her own life?'

'I'm in no position to suggest anything – yet. But we may get at the truth about many things if you were to ask Jane to call on Mrs Heseltine and give her the news. Women –'

'Sorry, but that can't be done.'

' – women have a flair for seeing through each other and it's possible . . . What did you say?'

'I thought I'd told you that Jane's been away for the past ten days. Some friends invited both of us to go cruising with them on the Lakes but I couldn't make it. I'm expecting her back early in the week.'

'That's a pity,' Quinn said. 'I mean, it's a pity she's out of town. How would you like to do it?'

'Not while I'm under the impression you're busy pushing the pieces around. Anyway, what do you think it would achieve?'

'To be frank, I'm not sure. But, if nothing else, Mrs Heseltine's reaction might be revealing when she hears that the pretty member of Dr Stone's team has gone the way of Pauline Gordon.'

'Why don't you go and tell her?'

'She doesn't know me . . . and I don't know her. Someone like you is much more suitable. Incidentally, it had better be done before the news gets out or it won't come as a surprise. And that would defeat the whole object.'

'If I knew what was going on in your tortuous mind I'd feel better in my own,' Piper said. 'All I'm prepared to do is phone her. If that's not good enough you'll have to find somebody else.'

Quinn grumbled, 'It's not good enough but it'll have to do. Ring me back when you've spoken to her, will you?'

'All right. But I wish I knew what you expect to get out of it.'

'For myself – ' Quinn felt no satisfaction at what he was thinking – 'perhaps nothing except the completion of a job of work. Perhaps not even that if I've been on a false trail all along. However, you may flatter me by saying I'm serving the cause of justice.'

Piper asked, 'For whom? Robert Heseltine?'

Etched on the background of Quinn's mind he could see a matchstick man suspended with outstretched arms and legs above the sea. That was something he understood. But the death of Christine Bowater demanded its own reckoning.

'No, not Heseltine,' Quinn said. 'For him, justice will come too late . . .'

CHAPTER XV

THERE WAS no reply from Lynn's number. Piper tried again after his solitary lunch and again later in the afternoon. By then he had come to the conclusion that she must still be in Dorchester, in all probability staying with Mrs Lloyd.

He spent a lazy day, his thoughts turning every once in a while to Quinn's final comment before he rang off. Even more insistent was an earlier remark.

'. . . *Well, now, that's the whole point. It's what he didn't tell me.*'

The trouble with Quinn was his practice of evasion. If he had explained what he and the detective-superintendent had talked about there would be something to get hold of. But all his talk gave no sort of hint. The area of conjecture was wide open.

And yet . . . He had said one positive thing. It was part of his allegation that Lynn might not have told the truth.

'. . . *I think we've been looking at this affair the wrong way round . . . Everybody assumed it was a case of an erring husband . . .*'

That lingered in Piper's thoughts. He went on hearing it until it was just a string of words with scarcely any meaning.

Then a recollection of something almost forgotten rose up from the depths of his memory. Once again Quinn was repeating what he had heard from Downey about a woman called Rose Lofthouse.

'. . . *She says the driver behaved like a man who was either blind or drunk. If she hadn't grabbed her dog and got close into the hedge he'd have run over her . . . From what she saw of him he looked like a zombie . . .*'

Two separate thoughts became one as though attracted

to each other in a magnetic field. Piper's mind froze as he realized the pattern that all the random bits and pieces now formed.

This must have been what Quinn meant. He, too, had guessed the truth. But it could be no more than a guess.

Lynn Heseltine would know the answer. That answer might well account for her admission that she was equally to blame for what had happened.

Piper hated to think how far her guilt extended, what part she had played in the events of Saturday, August 20. It must all have begun long before that night when a man had gone to his death in the waters of the English Channel.

There must also be a place into which Christine Bowater fitted. To believe she had taken her own life was asking too much. It could only be that she had stumbled on the secret behind Robert Heseltine's disappearance on the cliffs near Little Mallet.

No other explanation was tenable. She had shown nothing more than a touch of sadness when she talked about the day she came on duty.

'... Got here about a quarter to seven and saw Mr Heseltine driving away as I parked my car ... He seemed all right to me.'

What she must have discovered was bound to be the whole secret. Nothing less would account for her death.

Now Lynn Heseltine was safe. No one would ever suspect that she had been involved, that she was responsible for what had happened.

'... No one but you and Quinn. Whatever you might be tempted to do, nothing will stop him – to use his own words – serving the cause of justice. It's obvious now what he meant when he said that, for Heseltine, justice will come too late ...'

There was still no reply when Piper phoned Lynn's number at half past six. So he made himself a light meal and then sat watching the sun go down while he thought of a man travelling to destruction.

No one could possibly have known that a girl was destined to die because of what was about to happen when Robert reached the end of his journey. That was always the stuff of which tragedies were composed . . .

At nine o'clock, Piper tried again. This time Lynn answered.

She said, 'I've just come back from Dorchester. You know – about Robert, don't you?'

'Yes.' Although he felt like a hypocrite, Piper was forced to add, 'I'm sorry – very sorry. For the past week, I've been hoping there would be some other explanation.'

'So was I. Yet I seemed to know all the time that it was a foolish hope . . .'

Her voice broke. He disliked more than ever what he had to do but it was a duty he had no right to shirk.

He said, 'This isn't easy to talk about . . . but there's something I must tell you. I don't suppose you'll have heard about it yet.'

With an undercurrent of nervousness, she asked, 'Heard about what?'

'A girl called Christine Bowater . . . member of a surgical team at the Clinic. They're the ENT people who work for Mr Stone.'

Lynn said, 'I can't say that I know her. Of course, I've met Mr Stone once or twice . . . but why should you want to talk to me about this girl?'

'Because she's dead.' Without a pause, Piper went on, 'She was found in bed this morning with her wrist cut. There's no doubt in my mind that her death is linked with what happened to Robert.'

At the other end of the line there was a sound of anguished protest. Then Lynn cried out '. . . It's not true . . . it can't be true . . .'

She stopped as though fighting for breath. Piper remained quiet and waited.

It was a long wait. He could hear her crying like a

woman who had reached the ultimate in heartbreak. However much she was to blame he felt an overwhelming pity
for her.

She seemed to be talking to herself incoherently. None of
it made any sense to him until at last she began saying over
and over again '. . . My God . . . oh, my God . . . oh, my
God . . .'

Moments later he heard her fumbling with the telephone.
He wanted to comfort her but he knew that words no longer
had any meaning. Then she hung up and freed him from
the torment in her voice.

Quinn had gone out on an assignment. '. . . Should be
back in an hour or so. Will that be too late or do you want
him to ring you when he comes in?'

'Doesn't matter how late it is,' Piper said. 'Say I'll expect
to hear from him whatever time he gets back.'

Eleven o'clock came and went but there was still no call
from Quinn. By eleven-thirty Piper decided he might as
well go to bed. Quinn's day normally ended at midnight.
If he had been delayed it was more than likely he would go
straight home.

The flat was strangely quiet. It reminded Piper of those
lonely days long ago before he met Jane and changed the
whole pattern of his life.

. . . No man is fully alive who lives a solitary existence.
Women in the same circumstances are different. They seem
able to adapt. Now, for me, a mere couple of weeks is too
long. Time Jane came home. Glad it's only another two or
three days . . .

He knew this empty feeling of loneliness brought back
recollections of the bad days because he could still hear
Lynn Heseltine weeping and distracted on the phone. The
years ahead of her would be more lonely than anything he
had ever known.

His sense of guilt had been largely imagined. Hers would
demand a life-time of atonement.

Before he drew the bedroom curtains he stood for a while in the dark looking out at the serene calm of the summer night. The sky was clear, the stars like glittering specks of crystal. They had been there for five thousand million years, unheeding and uncaring. They never changed.

Men lived and men died but neither their achievements nor their failures altered the course of the stars journeying through eternal darkness. So much was futility, so many things without purpose or consequence.

A hundred years were nothing in the history of man. Yet in much less than a hundred years people like Robert Heseltine and his wife . . . Quinn . . . an unfortunate girl called Christine Bowater . . . Mrs Lloyd, who had innocently triggered off a deadly sequence of events . . . an unnamed GP who could not have guessed . . . all would be forgotten . . .

The phone bell cut through Piper's meditation. He groped his way to the bedside reading lamp, switched it on and picked up the receiver.

Quinn asked, 'Have I disturbed your chaste and peaceful slumbers?'

'No, I'm glad you phoned. I was feeling rather depressed.'

'Missing the missus?'

'Partly that, I suppose. The place isn't the same when she's away.'

'Bet she wouldn't like to think it was the same.'

'She knows better than that. Home isn't home without a wife.'

'You should set that to music,' Quinn said. 'And now let's change the subject before you start promoting the joys of matrimony. Spoken to Mrs Heseltine yet?'

'Yes. Didn't enjoy the experience, either.'

'What did she say when you told her about Dr Bowater?'

'Not much . . . but enough. Her reaction pretty well confirmed what you've been thinking.'

'Does that mean you think the same?'

'There would seem to be no other explanation. The difficulty will be to convince the police that it's anything more than guesswork.'

'May not be so difficult. Two things can't be ignored.'

'What two things?'

'Well, first of all, I doubt if they'll accept that Christine Bowater's death was suicide.'

'Probably not. And the second thing?'

Quinn said, 'My motive for making a trip to the cliffs where Heseltine disappeared.'

'Why did you go there?'

'Ah, you want to know too much.'

'Don't be silly. It can't be all that important.'

'You shock me to the marrow,' Quinn said. 'Since when did you start using expressions like "all that"? The influence of the advertising copy-writer seems to have no limits. If you mean "so important" it's so important that you say so. Now what were you asking?'

'Just a simple question. What's the second thing you're reluctant to tell me?'

'Something that's only important because it wasn't where it should've been. The rest you can think out for yourself. And that's my last word.'

'If it is, I never thought I'd live to see this day,' Piper said.

'Oh, clever stuff. Better get to bed before you strain yourself.'

With a horsey laugh, Quinn added, 'Sleep on it . . . as the actress said to the bishop. The answer's right in front of your eyes. When you've thought about it – '

'I don't need to,' Piper said. 'I'd already guessed it could be only one thing. All I wanted was confirmation. Now I'll say good night . . .'

He got down to the office before nine o'clock next morning. By half past ten he had cleared up the day's correspondence and arranged several appointments for later in the week.

More than once, thoughts of Lynn Heseltine disturbed him. He wondered what she would do with the knowledge she possessed and if she had the courage to take the only course open to her.

Perhaps she would try to forget her part in what had taken place on the day Robert's trip to Dorchester had been delayed. Perhaps she would try to persuade herself that what was done could not be undone. If she did, the secret of that Saturday night might well remain a secret for all time.

It depended to a great extent on her feelings for Robert. Nothing could change the past. If she tried to influence the future there was every prospect that she would destroy herself.

The choice was hers alone. Almost certainly she knew the truth. It had been in her voice when she cried out, '. . . *It's not true . . . it can't be true . . . My God . . . oh, my God . . . oh, my God . . .*'

Whether she would be willing to provide the proof of what she knew was another matter. That could take more than courage. That could add weight to the cross she would bear for the rest of her life.

He should do nothing more. Perhaps he had already done too much. Friendship for Robert Heseltine might demand too high a price. Now all he could do was wait for Lynn to decide.

A feeling of unease disturbed him – a feeling which grew stronger as time went by. Soon he realized it was fear. He could give no reason for being afraid but fear had gathered all around him like a physical presence.

There ought to be some action he should have taken. It must be wrong to leave things as they were, to let events take their own course. The situation would have to be resolved . . . one way or another.

While he was still trying to decide, his phone rang. Reluctance to answer it made him annoyed with himself. This desire to retreat from reality was childish . . .

Quinn asked, 'Are you alone?' He sounded far from his usual self.

'Yes. Why?'

'I'd like to come and see you . . . if you can spare a little while for a chat.'

'By all means. I suppose you want to talk about the Heseltine affair?'

'It ruined my night's sleep,' Quinn said. 'I had some nasty dreams and I've been carrying around a load of worry ever since I got out of bed.'

'What's worrying you?'

'Mrs Lynn Heseltine. She's in this business right up to the neck and I don't think much of her prospects. You and I ought to do something about it.'

'All right, I'll expect you inside the next half-hour,' Piper said.

He had plenty to do but there was no sense in trying to concentrate on office work. His fear was worse than ever. Now it had begun to close in on him.

The minutes passed slowly. He stood at the window looking down at the narrow confines of Vigo Street with its busy little shops and swarming traffic.

On the pavement outside the flower shop almost opposite there was a display of chrysanthemums and late roses and a variety of pot plants under the protective shade of a sun-blind. They had been newly-watered and they were a cool moist oasis in the dusty street.

Once upon a time that was where he had bought a bunch of flowers each year on the anniversary of Ann's death and taken it to Highgate cemetery. Now he no longer made his annual pilgrimage. The living had a duty to life. Ann would understand.

Every marriage had some day to come to an end. Every relationship became a memory. But not all were like Robert

and Lynn Heseltine. There something had gone wrong –
something that could never be put right. Many people got a
second chance . . . but not the Heseltines.

A greater tragedy was Christine Bowater. She had been
young and fresh, hardly beyond the real threshold of life.
Perhaps she, too, had made a mistake. If so, for her there
had been no second chance, either.

Facilis descensus Averni . . . The road to hell was all too
easy. After that first step few men could find the way back.

However great the crime, it was not for him to sit in
judgment. There was a saying : To understand all is to forgive all. He had no right either to forgive or to condemn.
He himself could only be grateful that he had been given
the chance to pick up the pieces and begin again . . .

Quinn arrived just before eleven o'clock. He looked as
he had sounded on the phone.

In a subdued voice, he said, 'I think it's about time we
stopped playing games. Whatever Lynn Heseltine may have
done, I don't want her to come to a sticky end. That girl
Bowater was bad enough. This thing mustn't be allowed to
go any further.'

'You can't stop it while you're only guessing,' Piper said.

'Those missing sunglasses are more than a guess. You
knew what I meant, didn't you?'

'Yes, I saw it when you told me the answer was right in
front of my eyes. That woman, Rose Lofthouse, never mentioned them . . . and I suppose Detective-Superintendent
Wainwright didn't, either?'

'Not a single reference. He gave me a detailed list of
everything they found in Heseltine's car, in his jacket on
the edge of the cliff and on the body picked up by the cargo
vessel *Sarah Lee*. No sunglasses anywhere. Yet Christine
Bowater had seen Heseltine wearing them when he drove
away from the Clinic. I remembered she'd told you that
herself.'

Piper recalled those moments in the corridor when he
had been introduced to her by Dr Egan. As she shook hands

she was a pretty girl with a pretty smile.

But there was no smile on her face when she talked about Robert Heseltine. It was as though she had known then the secret of his disappearance . . . although that was hardly possible.

'. . . *I was a short distance away from him and he was wearing his sunglasses . . . but he seemed all right to me . . . I hope nothing really bad has happened to him . . .*'

Quinn was saying '. . . It could mean only one thing. And after you phoned Mrs Heseltine last night, she knows. She must know . . . or I'm stark raving mad. It's the one explanation which fits the facts.'

'You still need proof that'll stand up in a court of law,' Piper said.

'Lynn Heseltine's got the proof . . . or what's near enough to it. And the thing I'm scared of is – '

The phone bell cut through Quinn's next word. With his mouth open he watched Piper reach for the receiver.

'Hello?'

At the other end there was no sound. Then Piper heard a voice he barely recognized.

'Is that you, John?'

'Yes. I was just about – '

'This is Lynn – Lynn Heseltine. You told me once that you wanted to help in any way you could. Well, I need your help now . . . I need it desperately. I must talk to you, John. Can you come here right away . . . please?'

Piper said, 'Of course. But until I get there don't open the door to anyone. I'll be as quick as I can because I think I've guessed what you want to tell me. So do as I say and don't let anyone in. Understand?'

As though she had not heard him, Lynn said, 'I know what happened to Robert. It's all my fault. When you phoned me last night I knew I was responsible for the whole thing. I'm the one who should've died instead of that girl at the hospital . . . and I wish I was dead. Oh, God, I wish I was dead . . .'

Then she hung up. The warm sunlight through the window felt cold as Piper looked at Quinn and said, 'It was Lynn Heseltine. She wants to see me . . . and all she can say is that she should be dead instead of Christine Bowater. I haven't the slightest doubt she means it, too. Like to come along?'

'Try and stop me,' Quinn said.

They had difficulty picking up a taxi. It was twenty minutes to twelve before they got to Martendale Crescent.

As they rounded the horse-shoe of detached houses Piper saw there was a car parked outside number 19 under the shade of a tree. One of the double gates was half-open.

He said, 'I was afraid of that. She didn't do as she was told.'

When he had paid off the driver, he added, 'I only hope we're in time . . .'

The taxi drove off as Quinn followed him up the paved drive. Martendale Crescent drowsed in the quiet sunshine again. There was no sign of life in number 19.

Inside the porch the air was heavy with the scent of summer flowers. Quinn had a momentary feeling that he was back in one of those long hot days of his childhood – the days that could never have been as perfect as memory pretended.

He watched Piper touch the bellpush lightly. In the silence all around them they listened to the chime of the bell.

It was the only sound throughout the house. Nothing stirred while it hung in the air, fainter and fainter, until everything was quiet once more.

Piper remembered that other time when he had stood outside Pauline Gordon's house and listened to the wailing of an old woman in the final throes of despair. Now the voice that filled his head was Lynn Heseltine saying '. . . *I wish I was dead . . . oh, God, I wish I was dead . . .*'

Behind him, Quinn asked, 'What now?'

As Piper reached out to the bellpush again there were small noises not far off. Footsteps came out of the distance and drew near – footsteps of someone forced to make the effort.

They were a woman's footsteps. He felt almost afraid of what the next few moments might reveal. When he glanced round he saw the same look on Quinn's face.

An awkward hand fumbled with the lock. It seemed to turn with difficulty. Then the door opened.

She was the same slim and elegant Lynn Heseltine whom he had known and admired ever since they first met. Not a strand of her sleek black hair was out of place, nothing marred her lovely features.

But one thing had changed. The last time he had been here, her wide dark eyes were filled with weariness. Now they were void of all emotion. The light had gone out of them. Now she seemed no more than the hollow wax figure of a beautiful woman.

Her voice was lifeless, too, as she said, 'I'm glad to see you, John. Come in.'

She had seen that Piper was not alone but she behaved as though Quinn were of no consequence, as though her mind had travelled far off. He felt that she was looking through him at some distant place.

When he followed Piper into the hall she made no protest. After she closed the front door she led them into the charming little room at the rear of the house where Piper had listened to her admission of guilt the last time he had visited number 19 Martendale Crescent.

This time there was neither guilt nor grief in her eyes as she turned, pale and erect, to face him. She said, 'I killed my husband. It's through me that it all happened.'

Piper said, 'You were the cause but not the instrument.'

'What – ' she sounded almost uncaring – 'what difference does that make?'

'The difference between life and death for a girl you

probably never knew. If you hadn't killed Robert, Christine Bowater would still be alive.'

'Don't make excuses for me. I'm to blame for that, too.'

'Only in the sense that none of this would've taken place if you hadn't betrayed him right at the start.'

With the ghost of something terrible at the back of her eyes, Lynn asked, 'How long have you known?'

'Since my friend here fitted a jumble of illogical pieces into a logical answer. It was the only answer that could explain why Robert's car should've been abandoned on the cliffs near Little Mallet.'

She looked at Quinn. In a wooden voice, she said, 'It's a pity you didn't find the answer sooner.'

Quinn said, 'I wish I had . . . but I couldn't. It wasn't until she was found dead that I realized the whole thing must've begun at the Brompton Clinic. If your husband had drowned in the English Channel, then he wasn't responsible for Dr Bowater's death. It had to be somebody else – somebody who was behind what happened that Saturday night. Otherwise none of it made sense.'

'What I did –' Lynn closed her eyes and shivered – 'didn't make sense, either . . .'

Numbness took hold of Piper while he listened. He wanted her to stop. He had no wish to hear this tortured woman strip her inner self naked.

'. . . I must've been mad to let him. Just once . . . oh, my God . . . just once. I'd give the rest of my life to cancel out that one day.'

'Perhaps you will sacrifice the rest of your life,' Piper said. 'Even in this permissive age, people are going to judge you harshly when the truth becomes known.'

'But how was I to know this would happen? How was I to know?'

There was no answer that Piper could think of. Quinn said, 'You couldn't anticipate that your husband would find out. I can't even guess how he learned he'd been betrayed by a medical colleague. But I don't need to guess that it must've been someone who had a professional relationship with you. Few other men would resort to killing to preserve their reputation.'

Lynn had nothing to say. When she stood dumb and stricken, Quinn asked, 'Who is your doctor, Mrs Heseltine?'

She shook her head. Piper knew that nothing mattered to her any more.

He said, 'Have you told him you're going to expose the whole affair?'

'Yes.' Her voice was as listless as the look in her eyes. 'I asked him to come here an hour ago . . . and we talked. He didn't deny any of it. He admitted everything.'

'You ran a very big risk.'

'No . . . he wouldn't harm me. What he did to Robert was forced on him. It might even be called an accident. I believe him when he says it just – just happened.'

'Christine Bowater's death was no accident.'

'Even –' Lynn clasped and unclasped her hands – 'even that I can understand. He panicked because she asked him why he'd left his car in the hospital car-park that Saturday night. She'd seen it there when she went to collect her own car . . . and she went back to look for him.'

'Why?'

'She – she wanted to invite him to go home with her.'

Quinn thought of Christine's abruptness on the phone. He had guessed right. Somebody was with her . . .

He said, 'Not for the first time either, I should imagine. Did you know about her?'

Lynn Heseltine moistened her lips. She said, 'Yes . . . but only after I'd made a fool of myself. It didn't matter, anyway. He meant nothing to me, then or since.'

She turned to look out at the sunlit garden. In the same dead voice, she added, 'What took place between us was just sheer insanity.'

'It's happened to other women,' Piper said. 'Perhaps

insanity is as good a word as any. But, in view of everything, didn't you think it could explain Robert's disappearance?'

'No.' She shook her head again. 'Not until you rang last
night and told me about Christine Bowater. Before then I
hadn't even known her name. But suddenly it came to me
in a flash. I could see it all as though I'd been in the car
when Robert left to go to Dorchester.'

Piper asked himself whether it made any difference —
true or false. He had no feeling for Lynn Heseltine. He only
wanted to get away from this house where the ghost of a
dead friendship still lingered. It would be the duty of other
people to lay that ghost.

He said, 'There was a car outside your gate when we got
here. Is it his?'

'Yes. He promised me he'd wait until I'd spoken to you.
At first he'd hoped I'd keep quiet but I refused to protect
him. Eventually he saw that he couldn't go on living with
himself whatever I did. It all had to come out.'

'Where is he now?'

'In the sitting-room. He won't run away . . . so there's no
hurry. I'd like you to know how it all began.'

'There's no need. We should be sending for the police
and —'

'Plenty of time,' Lynn said. 'You've been a friend of his
and you may be able to understand. I've got his written
confession. I want you to read it before you see him . . .'

CHAPTER XVI

"IT WAS NOT far off six o'clock when we met outside number 3 theatre. He said he had a couple of things to do and then he was off to Dorchester to visit a relation who was ill.

When I asked him if it were serious, he said, 'I don't really know. I'm having a consultation with her GP to see if we can sort out the cause of the trouble.'

I said, 'Hope it's nothing to worry about. Anyway, you've got a fine evening for the trip. Coming back tonight?'

'No. Bit too much for me after a busy week. I'll stay over at my aunt's place and return tomorrow morning.'

'Good idea. If this GP turns out to be an alarmist, you may even enjoy the fresh air and sunshine.'

'Not much chance of that. I hate driving on my own. Besides, I can't help feeling concerned for the old girl.'

'What seems to be wrong with her?'

'Not sure. Her doctor has described some conflicting symptoms. She's been suffering intermittently from vertigo, headache, nausea with vomiting, and diplopia. He thinks it might be a possible basilar artery syndrome.'

'Suppose it could be,' I said. 'What's your opinion?'

'Well, I suspect a space-occupying lesion in the brain. It fits all the symptoms.'

'So does a chronic middle-ear disease which may be non-discharging at the present time. I investigated a case like that three or four months ago.'

After he had thought about it, Robert asked, 'You doing anything special this weekend?'

I said, 'Not that I'm aware of. Why?'

'Oh, just been thinking. Like to do me a favour?'

'If I can.'

'Then how about coming along with me and taking a look at the old lady? I've got a high regard for her and I'd appreciate your opinion very much. Of course, I know it's asking a lot . . .'

The way he put it I could scarcely refuse. So I said, 'I've been mostly stuck indoors for the past week and I suppose a breath of fresh air won't do me any harm. Is there a spare bed at your aunt's house?'

'Yes, plenty of room. You'll be more than welcome.'

I said, 'All right. But you'll have to wait until I go home and pack some things.'

He told me that would take too long. It was getting late and we would save time if he loaned me whatever I might need. We wore the same size in shirts and he had brought two or three in his overnight bag as well as several pairs of socks. I could also borrow his electric razor on Sunday morning.

Well, I accepted his offer. Then I remembered I had left my *Telegraph* at home and I wanted to finish the X-word puzzle that I had started at breakfast time. I could probably get a copy from the newsagent's shop near the hospital because they stayed open late on a Saturday.

By that time he was almost ready to leave. So we arranged that I should go for my paper and he would pick me up on the corner.

That was what we did. On our way out of London we talked about various things and he mentioned that he was getting pretty annoyed with a woman patient he had operated on some months ago and who had begun sending him amorous letters. There seemed no way of stopping the nuisance.

I told him he should get one of the welfare people to call on her. He thought he might try that if she continued to badger him.

After a while we ran out of conversation. He concentrated on his driving and I turned to my X-word.

A few minutes later I saw him glance at my pen once or twice. He said it looked like one he had lost some months ago. I said I had lost several of them and I hoped it did not happen to this one.

He asked me if he might look at it. When I handed it to him he said it bore his monogram.

What happened after that is sheer nightmare. He told me he had done some writing in bed one night and discovered his pen was missing when he got to his consulting rooms next day. On returning home he had searched for it without success. The only explanation was that he must have lost it when he was getting out of his car.

Now it had turned up again and in my possession. At the time, he thought he had left it on his bedside table and it must have fallen on the floor. Now he was quite sure that was what had happened. And there was only one way I could have got hold of it. I had been in his bedroom and picked it up, thinking it was mine.

Of course, he was right but I tried to deny it. That afternoon long ago when I was getting dressed again I had seen what looked like my pen on the floor. I never noticed the tiny monogram from that day until Robert pointed it out to me. Since then I have found my own pen at the bottom of a pocket in a suit I seldom wear.

Well, all my denials got me nowhere. The more I argued the more certain he became.

Eventually, he said, 'I've suspected that something's been going on between you and my wife. Couldn't prove it before but I can now.'

I said, 'You're out of your mind. Better not let your wife hear you talk this way.'

'Oh, don't worry. She'll hear me, all right – and so will the GMC. When it all comes out in the divorce court, the Disciplinary Committee will know what to do with you. I'll drag you through the mire . . . just see if I don't.'

'You're making a terrible mistake. I can explain how I come to have your pen. You must've dropped it at the hospital and I imagined it was – '

'I'm not interested in your explanations. I'll get the truth out of her if it's the last thing I do. You can lie yourself black in the face but she won't. I'll know if she's lying.'

It was no use protesting any more. So I admitted everything. I told him it had all been over and done with long ago and that afternoon in the bedroom had been the only time.

He refused to believe me. He said I had ruined his marriage and now he was going to ruin my career. I was guilty of gross professional misconduct because I had been her doctor when I seduced her.

Perhaps I should not have argued any more. Perhaps I said something that pushed him too far. All I know is that he suddenly pulled into the side and ordered me out of the car.

If I had done as I was told a lot of things would be different now. But I refused. And that was when he struck at me.

I knocked his arm aside and hit back at him. It must have been a harder blow than I intended because he caught his head against the door pillar and blacked out.

When I tried to bring him round I realized he needed hospital treatment. So I pulled him out of the driving seat, made him as comfortable as I could and got behind the wheel myself.

All I intended was to take him to a hospital in Dorchester. Then I could arrange to come back to London. I swear that was my only thought.

Where the idea came from to get rid of him I shall never know. I tried to push it out of my mind but it kept returning. And at last I realized it was a case of Robert or me. With him out of the way I would be safe.

The rest was all too easy. I pulled into a side road, removed his cap and linen jacket and sunglasses, and put them on. He was still unconscious when I lifted him into the back of the car and laid him on the floor where he would not be seen.

I knew he must be suffering from serious brain damage and would probably not recover whatever I did. It is my only excuse for what I did from then on.

Before I reached Dorchester I had decided that the one way of disposing of him without starting a murder inquiry was to make it look like suicide. Once, when on holiday in Dorset, I had walked along the cliffs. There was no real alternative so I drove to that spot near Little Mallet.

After I had wiped the steering wheel and the door handles and everything else I could think of, I pressed Robert's hands on them to leave only his fingerprints in case the police checked. Then I placed his cap and jacket where they were found.

Last of all I carried him to the edge of the cliff and pushed him over. It was so easy, so damned easy.

I took my medical bag from the car and set off to walk to Winterbourne Abbas. I have no recollection of seeing anyone on the way and I doubt if anyone remembered seeing me.

At Winterbourne Abbas I caught a late bus to Dorchester. I stayed at a hotel that night under a false name and next morning went by train to London.

When I got home I shaved and changed and then took a taxi to the Clinic. After making a pretence of looking in on one or two patients I collected my car from the hospital car-park . . .

It was a couple of days later when I found his sunglasses in the outside breast pocket of the jacket I had worn that night. I always keep mine in that pocket and I must have put his there without thinking. I got rid of them down a street drain the same night.

His pen should have been somewhere in the car but apparently the police never found it. I can only assume it went out of the window as he fell back when I struck him.

I am not sorry now for what I did. My only regret is that Christine had to be killed.

If she had not wanted to know why I had left my car in the hospital grounds that night and where I had gone, everything would have been all right. But she went on asking questions and I knew she would eventually suspect the truth. So I had to say I would explain later.

She fell asleep after we had made love. I hated myself but it had to be done. I put my pillow over her face and lay across her so she could not scream out. Then I cut her wrist with a razor blade.

There was hardly any struggle. She lost consciousness very quickly. Before I left her flat she was dead.

It was all just like the death of that woman Pauline Gordon who had pestered Robert. She was a real depressive and I felt no surprise when I heard what had happened to her. If anything, I was glad. People would think she had committed suicide because there had been an affaire between Robert and her.

I want no one to blame Lynn. From start to finish the fault was all mine. If only I had met her before she married Robert . . .

Now I have told the whole story. Regret is futile. The past canot be changed. Now there is only one price I can pay for what I have done."

The house was silent again when Piper came to the end. As he folded the half-dozen sheets of paper he saw the look of aversion on Quinn's face. Lynn Heseltine showed no emotion at all.

In a wooden voice, she said, 'I'll take you to see him.'

She walked ahead of them to a room across the hall. With a tired gesture she pointed to the door. Then she turned and left them.

They went inside a room where the curtains were half drawn to keep out the sun. The light was poor but they could see all they needed to see.

Quinn said, 'I thought that would be the price he'd want to pay.'

Dr Egan was lying slumped in an armchair, his head resting against its high back, his eyes closed. He looked like a man relaxed in sleep.

On the floor beside him lay an unstoppered bottle. Piper caught a whiff of a sweet penetrating odour that he had smelled once before.

'I can smell it, too,' Quinn said. 'I've heard of the stuff. If I'm right and it is hydrocyanic acid, he'd be dead before he had time to replace the stopper.'

The chain of tragedy that had bound so many people together in death soured Piper's thoughts. Even the touch of the papers he was holding felt unpleasant. He never wanted to see Lynn Heseltine again. She might have been more sinned against than sinning but he never wanted to see her again.

Quinn was saying '. . . Maybe just as well. Only the lawyers benefit from this kind of murder trial.'

'You take too practical a view for my liking,' Piper said. 'All I can think of is that the profession has lost a couple of damn' fine medical men just because one of them made a fool of himself over a woman. Better go and phone the police . . .'

CHAPTER XVII

A TRAFFIC HOLD-UP delayed his taxi on the way to Fleet
Street. It was ten minutes to three before he got to the
Three Feathers.

By that time most of the customers had gone and there
were only a few people in the lounge. Quinn was alone at
the end of the long bar, his hands around a half-empty
glass of bitter.

He looked up and grinned. He said, 'Better late than
never . . . as the bunny-girl said to the curate. I'd just
resigned myself to making these few mouthfuls of beer last
until closing time. Freddie!'

The barman limped towards them, his weasel face crumpled in a frown until he recognized Piper. Then he smiled
and said, 'Ah, good to see you, sir . . . even if you aren't
too particular about the company you keep. What may I
have the pleasure of providing for your sustenance?'

Quinn said, 'You've just talked yourself out of that half-
pint I'm always promising you. My friend will have a
double whisky and I'll have another pint of the usual.'

'Could that mean – could that conceivably mean –
you're paying?'

'But of course. Am I not known as the last of the big
spenders?'

With a blank look in his eyes, Freddie said, 'I never
thought I'd live to see this day. Double whiskies . . . I must
be hearing things.'

He brought the order and went away shaking his head
when Quinn paid him the exact amount. Piper asked, 'Are
we celebrating something?'

'But indeed.' Quinn finished his half-empty glass and
pushed it aside to make room for the new pint. 'I got a
fatherly pat on the back this morning from no less a person-

age than the managing editor himself. Seems he was quite taken by my column on the Heseltine affair.'

'I'm glad one of us is happy,' Piper said.

He poured some water into his whisky, took a drink and added, 'I'll need more than this stuff to get rid of the nasty taste in my mouth.'

'Well, that's understandable. Like one of your medical friends, you were emotionally involved. I had the advantage of being on the outside all along.'

Quinn swallowed a mouthful of beer and smacked his lips. He said, 'Between you and me and Brigid's bosom, I don't deserve any accolade for my share in the outcome.'

'Why not? It was you who saw the answer.'

'Maybe. But if I'd been a bit quicker – and I can't see yet why I wasn't – I might've saved a lassie who wanted to know more than was good for her.'

'You're not to blame for that,' Piper said.

'Pity all the same. I wanted to ask Mrs H. where she was on a certain Saturday night. Instead, I should've asked somebody else. I've no excuse when I remember thinking we might've got the whole thing wrong way round. The one we thought was being blackmailed had actually done the blackmailing himself.'

'Not quite. There was no blackmail involved.'

'Near enough,' Quinn said. 'Telling a professional man you'll have him struck off the medical register amounts to much the same thing. Self-preservation is a pretty strong motive if the opportunity comes his way.'

'Once, perhaps – but not twice.'

'Never having been in that position, I wouldn't know. However, some men might consider they'd gone too far to turn back. Funny . . . when you come to think of it.'

'What is?'

'The whole thing was triggered off by a blow struck in anger. No use conjecturing what might have happened if it had been aimed better . . . but in the event you might almost say it was self-defence.'

'You might,' Piper said. 'I wouldn't. That account of what took place was a bit too glib for my money.'

'Could be.' Quinn swallowed a long drink that almost emptied his glass.

When he put it down he let out a sigh of satisfaction and added, 'A man called William Cowper said that the truth lies somewhere, if we knew but where. Well, we won't ever know. And it doesn't matter now, anyway. A more important quotation right now is the one about Time's wingèd chariot hurrying near. Take a look at the clock above the bar. Freddie!'

The barman cupped a hand round his ear and turned slowly. He said, 'I hear a voice. Can it be? Why, yes it is. To think I should – '

'Keep the soliloquy until after closing time,' Quinn said. 'Mr Piper wishes to order the same again.'

'No more for me,' Piper said. 'But you have whatever you want. Incidentally, Jane's coming home this evening. I spoke to her on the phone last night and told her about the Heseltine affair . . . at least, my small part in it. She'd like very much to hear your side of the story.'

'Nothing to tell. I just made a lucky guess.'

'That's false modesty.'

'All right. Call it the old touch of genius. How do I explain to your dear wife the workings of a super mind?'

'You can try. She wants you to let her know when you'll be free to have dinner with us.'

A voice in Quinn's mind grumbled '. . . *Here we go again. She invites me for Piper's sake and I wriggle out of the invitation for Piper's sake. This interest of hers in the Heseltine affair is just a lot of malarkey – just an excuse. She knows you won't accept. What's more, she knows that you know she knows . . .'*

Freddie brought a fresh pint of bitter, acknowledged Piper's tip with an exaggerated salute and went away. Someone in the public bar called out 'Last orders, please. Any more for any more?'

'. . . *And maybe she also knows I envy my friend —
in the nicest possible way, of course. He deserves his happi-
ness . . . and I'm not going to spoil it by embarrassing
him . . .*'

Quinn raised his glass in a toast. He said, 'Here's to you
and Jane. Thank her for me and say I'll be grateful if she'll
make our dinner engagement an open date.'

'Wish I had a pound for every time I've heard you say
that,' Piper said.

'One of these days —' Quinn savoured a mouthful of
bitter before swallowing it — 'you'll get a surprise. Mean-
while, take care of yourself. As the virgin said to the sailor,
there aren't many of us left . . .'